Invitations to Personal Reading, Set B
Curriculum Foundation Classroom Library
Scott, Foresman and Company

Realistic Stories	
Blue Canyon Horse	Ann Nolan Clark
The Bus Trip	Eleanor Frances Lattimore
Chie and the Sports Day	Masako Matsuno
Judy's Journey*	Lois Lenski
Otis Spofford	Beverly Cleary

Biography and Historical Fiction	
Buffalo Bill	Ingri and Edgar Parin d'Aulaire
Copper-Toed Boots	Marguerite de Angeli
Crazy Horse: Sioux Warrior	Enid LaMonte Meadowcroft
The First Book of the Early Settlers	Louise Dickinson Rich
Lee, the Gallant General	Jeanette Eaton

Fun, Fancy, and Adventure	
Basil of Baker Street	Eve Titus
Dorrie and the Weather-Box	Patricia Coombs
The Dwarf Pine Tree	Betty Jean Lifton
Miss Osborne-the-Mop	Wilson Gage
The Perfect Pitch	Beman Lord

Books of Information	
About Policemen Around the World	Les Landin
Mr. Peaceable Paints	Leonard Weisgard
Spike, the Story of a Whitetail Deer	Robert M. McClung
Rusty Rings a Bell	Franklyn M. Branley and Eleanor K. Vaughan
Wonders of an Oceanarium	Lou Jacobs, Jr.

Books Too Good to Miss	
Adventure at Mont-Saint-Michel	Napoli
Favorite Fairy Tales Told in Germany*	retold by Virginia Haviland
Miss Happiness and Miss Flower	Rumer Godden
Once Upon a Horse	Arnold Spilka
The World Is Round	Anthony Ravielli

*Not included in sets for distribution in the British Commonwealth (except Canada).

MISS OSBORNE-THE-MOP

Miss

Osborne-the-Mop

by Mary Q. Steele

(WILSON N. GAGE, pseud.)

Illustrated by Paul Galdone

THE WORLD PUBLISHING COMPANY

CLEVELAND AND NEW YORK

Special Scott, Foresman and Company E
for the Invitations to Personal Reading Pr

Published by The World Publishing Company
2231 West 110th Street, Cleveland 2, Ohio

Published simultaneously in Canada by
Nelson, Foster & Scott Ltd.

Library of Congress Catalog Card Number: 63-8912

This edition is printed and distributed by Scott, Foresman and Company
by special arrangement with The World Publishing Company.

For my sister, EMMY WEST,
with love and admiration
and to commemorate the day she saw
the eastern meadowlark

MISS OSBORNE-THE-MOP

Chapter One

Dill Tracy crouched on top of a rock and watched the door to his house. It was a big old gaunt gray house, shabby and weathered. But he had spent every summer of his life in it and it seemed like a very nice house to him.

He was wearing shorts and sneakers and nothing else. The sun was very hot on the backs of his legs. He shifted his position a little, and a big blue-tailed lizard which had joined him on the warm rock skittered lightly away.

Dill was eleven years old. His name was John Pickett Tracy, Jr., but he had been christened Dill Pickle by some of his cousins, who took a dim view of him and felt this was a more appropriate name

than John Pickett. This had all happened such ages
ago, and he had been called Dill so long that now
almost nobody remembered he had any other name.

Dill didn't mind. He didn't mind anything much,
for he was a busy, good-natured boy. But right now
he minded something, and that was why he was
watching the house. What he minded was his cousin,
Jody Ransom, who was spending the summer with
him. Jody was just awful. She spent all her time
crying—everything made her cry. He bet she was
inside crying now.

If she came out of the house with a picnic basket,
he'd join her. There was hardly anything to cry
about on a picnic, and besides he was starving. But
if she came out empty-handed, he'd slide down off
that rock and sneak away without her. He had had
all the tears he meant to put up with for a while.

Inside the house, Jody was in truth about to cry.

"Jody," said Mrs. Tracy, "wouldn't you like to
pack a lunch and take it down by the creek and
have a picnic with Dill?"

"Yes'm," answered Jody glumly. "I guess I
would."

"Well, wouldn't you like to come out in the
kitchen and help me make sandwiches?" suggested
Mrs. Tracy. "We could use the ham left over from
supper last night, and I'll hard-boil some eggs."

Jody sighed. "All right, Aunt Margaret," she

agreed sadly, and she followed Mrs. Tracy out into the kitchen.

While Mrs. Tracy got out the ham and the mayonnaise and bread and put the eggs in a pan to boil, she glanced every now and then at her niece's gloomy face.

"Spread mayonnaise on the bread, and mustard if you want it, while I slice the ham," Mrs. Tracy directed.

Jody sighed again and began to unscrew the lid from the mayonnaise jar. "One sandwich is enough for me," she said drearily. Jody was inclined to be plump and was always making desperate resolves not to eat more than the barest minimum.

"All right," said Mrs. Tracy with a nod. "But how about cake? You know Dill will want some of that chocolate cake."

"A big piece for Dill and . . . and just a little piece for me," Jody said. She had seen the cake Aunt Margaret had made that morning, with nuts sprinkled thickly all over the swirling chocolate icing. It looked delicious—and fattening.

Mrs. Tracy began to put lettuce and ham on the slices of bread, and Jody wrapped each sandwich in wax paper. Between sandwiches she stared out the window where rhododendron pressed up against the panes and made the big kitchen, with its scrubbed old tables and counter, look rather dark and gloomy in spite of the white electric stove gleaming in one corner.

This whole house is gloomy, Jody thought. I used to love the way it seemed so sort of ramshackle and old-fashioned. But now it just seems dark and gloomy.

And when Aunt Margaret went into the pantry to get the cake, Jody sniffed deeply and then put out her tongue to catch a tear that rolled down her nose because she just couldn't hold it back.

If things hadn't started out so well, Jody told herself; if it hadn't looked as if it would be such a perfect summer, it might not seem so awful now. But a whole month at the seashore had sounded so blissful, especially since they were all going to be there together, Mother and Daddy and Jody and her two older brothers, Steve and Roger.

And then everything had begun to happen. The glasses had been first. Jody could never figure out why in the world Mother had taken her to the oculist. She didn't *feel* as if she was blinking and squinting. Dr. Green was a nice man, but she didn't like having all those lights shined in her eyes, and reading all those very dull charts.

"Just a muscular weakness," Dr. Green had said finally. "We'll soon straighten it out." And then he had said Jody must wear glasses all summer.

"All summer!" squealed Jody.

"Why, that's a short time," answered Dr. Green in surprise. "It'll be over in no time."

That wasn't the point, of course. It was bad enough to have to wear glasses at all, but worse when you meant to spend your days running up and down the sand and in and out of the ocean. You'd always have to be worrying about breaking them or losing them or something.

And then to make matters even more unpleasant, Dr. Green had given her the frames.

"You won't be wearing glasses permanently," he explained. "No need to buy frames. I'll just lend you these and at the end of the summer you can give them back."

So now they perched on Jody's nose, round and black and heavy and horrible. "They make me look like an owl," she complained. "A fat owl!"

And then Daddy had a chance to go to Europe on an assignment from a magazine. "I can't turn it down," he explained patiently to Jody. "With both Roger and Steve in college next fall, we'll need the money."

Jody's summer dwindled before her eyes. Because Roger found he could get a job that paid more than the job he had planned to take at the beach. And Steve's old camp director wrote and begged Steve to come back one last time as junior counselor before he went off to college. And Steve went.

Even then Jody and Mother could have gone to
the beach together and enjoyed the ocean and had
fun. But what happened? Grandmother got sick.
And naturally Mother had to go take care of her.

"Lamb, I know it's a disappointment to you,"
Mother said soothingly while Jody sobbed over this
last bit of bad news. "All of us have been disap-
pointed. This isn't what any of us had planned on,
and especially not poor Grandmother. And you're
lucky to have such a nice place to spend your vacation. You'll have lots of good times with Aunt Margaret and Uncle John and Dill."

Jody stared. Her mother must be out of her mind
to think that anybody could have fun with horrible
Dill. It was pretty and pleasant up in the North
Carolina mountains, but Dill— Ugh!

And it was turning out to be just as bad as she
had expected, or maybe worse. Even the books she
had brought to read made her head ache because
of the glasses.

And who wanted to go on a picnic with nasty Dill
when she might have been swimming at the beach
with Roger and Steve?

Aunt Margaret finished packing the basket and
handed it to Jody. "Poor love," she said and patted
her niece on the cheek. "I do hope you have fun."

Jody managed a frail smile. She was a little bit
ashamed. She should really try to be more cheerful

for Aunt Margaret's sake. After all, Aunt Margaret had troubles of her own—she was the mother of that ghastly Dill.

It was a bright June day. The path that led to the creek twisted among hemlocks and laurel bushes and great gray rocks. Jody took a big breath of the clear air, spicy with the smell of sun-warmed leaves and needles.

"For Pete's sake, are you crying again?" asked Dill, jumping off his rock.

Jody didn't answer. She bit her lip and hoped she didn't get so mad at Dill she really did cry. She walked on, keeping her eyes on the path and trying to think of something pleasant.

"Let's don't go that way," Dill called. "Let's go around by the bluff."

"It's longer by the bluff," objected Jody.

"But there's something interesting I want to show you there," Dill explained. "Aw, come on, Jody!"

"Oh, all right," agreed Jody grudgingly. "But you'll have to carry the basket."

Dill backed off with his hands behind him. "How can I show you the interesting thing with my hands full?" he cried.

Jody glowered. Dill hastily thought better of it. "You carry it to the interesting thing," he proposed, "and I'll carry it from there to the creek. That's about halfway, honest, Jody."

Jody considered. She wouldn't mind seeing an interesting thing. "Do you promise?" she asked at last. One thing about Dill, he never went back on a promise.

"Cross my heart," he answered cheerfully. So they took the path around by the bluff.

The day was warm in spite of the breeze that rustled in and out of the gnarled rhododendron bushes. Jody switched the basket from one arm to the other.

"When are we going to get to this thing?" she asked grimly.

Dill was jumping up on a rock. He always leaped around like a mountain goat. Jody couldn't understand why he wasn't continually in casts and splints. As his father often said, nobody missed better opportunities to break a leg than Dill.

"It's just around the bend, I think," he answered, jumping down. He ran ahead and disappeared into the bushes, thrashed around for a minute, and finally yelled, "We must've passed it. I can't find it. . . . Oh, no, here it is!"

Dragging the basket, Jody walked slowly to the spot. There on the ground was a horrid-looking black lump of something.

"What is it?" she asked impatiently.

"It's a dead rabbit," said Dill, poking it with a stick. "Or anyway it was the other day."

"Oh, ugh!" wailed Jody. "Dill, you're horrible! I came all this way because you said it was something interesting. Oh, you're mean!"

"Why?" asked Dill, surprised. "I think it's very interesting. Look, there's its skull."

Jody let the basket fall and put her hands over her eyes, or rather over her glasses.

"Oh, all right," said Dill in disgust. He dropped the stick and picked up the basket. "Come on!"

He ran on down the path. Jody stood a minute, trying hard not to cry. Then she followed slowly. She wished she hadn't let him carry the lunch. The way he was jumping around, it would be nothing but crumbs by the time they reached the creek.

But it wasn't. It was in pretty good shape. Jody poured the tart, cold lemonade into two pink plastic cups, and handed Dill his sandwiches and hard-boiled eggs. Then she settled back against a tree and chewed her single sandwich slowly to make it last longer.

A picnic was fun, especially here in the cool shade by the creek. The water poured smoothly over a ledge of rock and fell into the pool below with a lovely hollow gurgle. The hemlocks leaned over their own reflections, and across the stream big white heads of rhododendron bobbed and nodded.

"Look at that squirrel," said Dill, busily cracking the shell of a hard-boiled egg. "Looky the way he

can run along the branches like that. Squirrels are
neat. And can they ever jump! It must be fun to be
a squirrel."

Jody looked up to where the squirrel peered down
at them from its tree. It gave its tail a brisk whisk
or two, like a feather duster, and then ran and
leaped out into space, seizing the tip end of a thin
branch that bent far down under its weight.

Jody sipped her lemonade. It would be fun to
live up in the leafy tree tops. But she'd rather be a
bird, come to think of it.

Up here in the mountains there didn't seem to be
many birds. But that was a bird singing now, wasn't
it? She strained to hear over the noise of the water
and of Dill's talking on and on about squirrels.

The song seemed to be coming from the rhododendron, a mysterious and lovely song, swirling
down and down, like the creek spilling over rocks.
If only Dill would be quiet!

"Don't crack your eggs so loud," she cried.

"I'm not cracking eggs," he answered indignantly.
"I'm eating cake. That's my teeth crunching nuts.
I like nuts on a cake. And in a candy bar. And even
in—"

"Will you be quiet?" Jody whispered fiercely.
The song had begun to die away.

"I guess squirrels are lucky," went on Dill as
though he hadn't heard. "Always jumping and eat-

ing nuts. That's about all they eat, you know, nuts like hickory nuts . . ."

The song had stopped. Jody turned angrily on Dill.

"Oh, you!" she cried helplessly. She gave him a furious look. "Oh, shut up and *be* a squirrel, will you? I—I—"

She broke off. The sound of the water swelled and faded all around her. The breeze bent the white racemes of rhododendron flowers back and forth among the leathery leaves. Jody stared.

For Dill was gone. And there, next to the ball of crushed wax paper which had held his slice of cake, sat a small gray squirrel!

Chapter Two

The squirrel uttered a rasping cough and made a leap for the trunk against which Jody was leaning. With a great scrabbling and scratching of claws it climbed straight up the tree, ran along a limb, leaped lightly into the next hemlock, and disappeared.

Slowly Jody shut her mouth, which had been hanging open in astonishment. She stared once again at the crumpled ball of wax paper. After a minute she jumped up and looked wildly about her. "Dill!" she shouted. "Dill, where are you? Come back! Come back!"

Her words echoed away among the rocks and smothered into the hemlock branches. And from somewhere far off that bird sang an answer in its cool flutelike voice, lovely and tantalizing.

Jody put her hands over her ears to shut out the sound. She felt dizzy, so she sat down on a rock and drew a deep breath. It was a joke, she decided. Dill was hiding somewhere and playing a trick on her. It was the kind of mean thing he would do.

But it couldn't be a joke. With her own eyes she had seen it. She had seen Dill sitting there beside her, and then the next instant Dill was gone and there were the squirrel and the wax paper.

But people didn't turn into squirrels. It was impossible. She must have been dreaming. She'd fallen asleep suddenly. Or perhaps she was still asleep. She got up and went to the edge of the stream and wet her handkerchief. The cold water felt good on her hot cheeks and forehead. Surely she must be awake. She leaned over and looked at her reflection, her round face and short dark hair. Well, anyway *she* wasn't a squirrel. She was still Joan Ransom, aged eleven and too fat. She sighed and sat down again.

After a while she felt better. It just couldn't have happened, it just couldn't. She must have dreamed it, and Dill had sneaked off while she was asleep.

It took her nearly an hour to decide this. When she had made up her mind, she packed the basket, carefully picking up all the scraps of paper and the plastic cups and the thermos bottle.

"Well," she said loudly in case Dill was hiding close enough to hear her, "it's nice out here, but I

guess I'd better go back. Aunt Margaret will be won-
dering what has become of me."

She paused and listened. The water chuckled. The
wind stirred among the tree tops, and that was all.
Jody tried to look calm and collected as she set off
toward the house. She took the short path, not the
one by the bluff and the interesting thing. As she
walked she strained her ears for the sound of Dill's
footsteps behind her or a rustle in the undergrowth
as he skirted the path beside her. But her own heart
pounded so loud in her ears she couldn't hear anything else.

In the kitchen she set the basket down on the
table. She put the thermos and the cups in the sink
and filled them with cool water to soak. Then she
tiptoed upstairs to her room. Perhaps Aunt Margaret was taking a nap. It wouldn't do to disturb
her.

Jody lay down herself and stared at the cracked
plaster on the ceiling. One of the cracks curled up
and around and in on itself, like a . . . like a squirrel's tail. Quickly Jody flounced over and gazed at
the chest of drawers that held her clothes. On top
of the chest sat her battered old teddy bear, Bruin.
He gazed back at her with his one button eye. What
a round black eye it was, like a squirrel's eye! Jody
jumped up and ran to the window.

From up here she could see almost down to the

creek. There wasn't any sign of Dill, or any squirrels, either. But far off, over the bluff, a big hawk
circled slowly in the sun.

Jody's stomach knotted up still further. Didn't
hawks eat squirrels? Suppose she really had turned
Dill into a squirrel, and suppose a hawk ate him?
Her throat was so dry she couldn't swallow and her
hands trembled.

Oh, Dill, she cried silently. Come back, come
back. I'll forgive you for everything, even the hat.
The hat was a wide-brimmed straw hat Aunt Margaret had given Jody to keep off the sun. But when
she first put it on, Dill had laughed so hard he had
literally fallen down and rolled around on the floor.
"Y–you look like some kind of cr–crab peering out
of its sh–shell," he gasped. "With that hat and those
g–g–glasses."

So she hadn't worn the hat again. But now she
felt she could forgive Dill even if she got a sunstroke
and had to spend the rest of this wretched summer
in bed, if he would only come running up the stairs,
right this minute.

At last she went back to her bed and took a book
from the table beside it. And for the next hour she
read. At least her eyes moved over the lines of print,
and her hands turned the pages; but afterward she
couldn't remember a word of it.

"Didn't Dill come home with you?" asked Aunt Margaret, suddenly appearing in the doorway.

"No'm," answered Jody, closing her book. "I—I think I saw him climbing a tree."

Suppose Aunt Margaret had asked, "Do you know what has happened to Dill?" What in the world would she say if Jody replied, "I turned him into a squirrel." Could you be arrested for turning people into squirrels? And suppose a hawk ate them, or a snake? Could you be accused of murder?

Jody didn't like to think of even horrible Dill being swallowed by a snake.

"Well," said Aunt Margaret, "I hope he gets back soon. I want him to go over to the Rabuns' and get some eggs for breakfast." And to Jody's relief she turned and went downstairs without saying anything more.

But of course this was only putting off the evil moment. Sooner or later someone was going to ask, "What has become of Dill?" And she would have to tell. She would have cried, only she was too miserable.

She was so miserable she hardly heard the scratching at first. Gradually it dawned on her that something was clawing frantically at the wire screen in her window. She turned her head. Something small and furry was crouching on the sill.

Slowly Jody got up from bed and crept to the window.

The squirrel pressed its face against the screening and gave her a pleading look. Jody looked fearfully back. The squirrel began to pluck impatiently at the wires. After a minute Jody unhooked the screen, shoved it open, and the squirrel squeezed in.

Was it really Dill? Jody's head whirled. The squirrel jumped to the floor, bounced around sideways, and rasped out a very bad word in squirrel language. It must be Dill, Jody decided.

She pressed her hands to her cheeks. What in the world was she going to do? She could hardly walk up to Aunt Margaret and hand her a squirrel and say, "This is your little boy, Dill."

How in the world had she done this thing to begin with. She hadn't really meant to do it. She'd only said, "Be a squirrel." She certainly hadn't dreamed it would come true. And oh, if only now the squirrel would be Dill!

She gazed into the little animal's eyes. Was it really Dill? "Oh, be Dill," she pleaded tearfully. "Be Dill again, please!"

There was a sort of flash, a swishing noise, and there stood Dill! She hadn't dreamed she'd ever be so glad to see him. Dear beautiful brown mosquito-bitten half-naked horrible darling Dill!

He shook himself all over, scratched behind one

ear, and said, "Gee, thanks." And before Jody could
open her mouth, he scooted out of the room. She
stared after him. Had it really happened? Had any
of it really happened?

She got up on her bed and began to read deter-
minedly. She couldn't bear to think about the last
few hours. It had all been some kind of crazy dream.
It must have been. It couldn't be true.

At supper Dill seemed unusually quiet. He
yawned a lot.

"You must have had a strenuous day," Uncle John
remarked.

"I think he spent the afternoon climbing trees,"
Aunt Margaret said. Dill shot her an astonished
look. "I expect shortly he'll grow a bushy tail and
start living in trees and eating nuts."

"No, thanks," said Dill fervently, "not me." And
he went to bed almost as soon as it got dark. But
Jody sat up late, reading. She wanted to be able to
sleep as soon as her head hit the pillow—and she
didn't want to have any crazy dreams.

When she woke, she'd forgotten the whole thing.
It wasn't till Dill sat down beside her at the breakfast table that she remembered any of it. What a
silly dream! She slid her eyes toward Dill, calmly
eating toast and strawberry jam. You couldn't spend

half a day as a squirrel and then sit at the breakfast table and eat like that, could you?

Dill drank his milk in gulps. Out in the kitchen Aunt Margaret was whistling, "You Ain't Nothin' but a Hound Dog," a song she much admired. Uncle John had long since gone off to his work, which was teaching history at the university in town.

Dill set his glass down and turned to Jody. "Gee, that was neat," he said suddenly. "How'd you do it?"

Jody turned red. "I don't know what you're talking about," she whispered fiercely. "I didn't do anything."

"Listen," Dill went on as if she hadn't spoken, "does it work on anything? I mean, could you change this plate into a squirrel? Or does it have to be alive?"

Jody drew back. "I can't change anything into anything," she said firmly. "That was a dream or a trick or something."

"For Pete's sake, Jody, what's the matter with you?" cried Dill. "I was a squirrel all afternoon. I guess I ought to know."

Jody looked at him curiously. "Was it fun?" she asked at last.

Dill considered. "Some of it was," he answered. "It was fun being able to climb trees and jump like that. But once I missed and fell about twenty feet.

And the other squirrels didn't like me much; they kept chasing me. And the only nuts I could find were acorns and they tasted terrible. And there were other things." He scratched reminiscently.

"Children, if you're through eating, bring your plates out here and then go make your beds," Aunt Margaret called. Jody obediently stood up and began to pile forks and spoons on her plate. Dill caught her arm.

"Meet me on the side porch when you get your bed made," he whispered. "And don't be a dope, Jody. We can really have some fun with this if you don't act like a dope."

The side porch was screened. There were some old rockers out there, and a rickety table with a lamp and some magazines on it, and a canvas folding chair that collapsed nine times out of ten when anybody sat in it. Dill was just sitting down in it, very carefully, when Jody came out. As soon as he saw her he jumped up without being careful, and it took them five minutes to get Dill and the chair untangled.

"The way I figure it," he told Jody as he drew one of his legs out from between the canvas and the wooden frame, "there's something radioactive about you, or something. You know, everything's made out of atoms; it's just that they're arranged different ways to make a bush and a person and a kitchen

stove. Well, somehow you've got the power to re-
arrange atoms to make what you want to out of
them. See?"

"You mean magic?" asked Jody. "I believe in
magic in books—some of my favorite books are magic
books. But I don't think it ever really happens to
real people."

"Don't be so stupid," cried Dill. "I'm not talking
about magic; I'm talking about science. And it
doesn't make any difference whether you believe in
it or not. You did it and that proves it."

"It . . . it was an accident or something," said
Jody, looking miserable. "I couldn't do it again."

"Sure you can," Dill told her. He picked up a
magazine from the table. "Here, make this be a
cake. With orange icing and nuts in it."

"Be a cake," said Jody fearfully, glaring at the
magazine. Nothing happened. "See, I told you," she
exclaimed triumphantly.

"You didn't try," complained Dill. "Aw, come on,
Jody! If I could do it, you can just bet I would.
Think of all the fun we can have with this. Now,
just try. Don't you want some cake? A big beautiful
three-layer cake with lots of nuts and real thick
icing with real orange juice. One like Steve had for
his birthday last year, remember?"

Jody did remember. A delicious cake with green-
and-white icing daisies around the sides. Orange ic-

ing was her favorite. She could almost smell the
fragrant orange juice. She could almost see the knife
sliding into it. "Be a cake," she whispered. And
there in Dill's hands, instead of the dull-looking
little magazine, was a big glistening three-layer cake,
complete with orange icing and daisies. On a plate,
too, just like her mother's cake plate.

"Yikes," said Dill in an awe-struck voice. He set
the cake gently on the table. "You did it."

He walked slowly around the table, inspecting
the cake from all sides. Jody closed her eyes and
thought. It couldn't happen. But when she looked
again, there it was. Dill was bending over it, sniffing
deeply. He reached out a cautious finger and touched
the icing. Then he licked the finger dreamily.

"It's real," he said at last. "I'll get a knife."

He vanished into the house and reappeared in a
minute with a knife and two saucers. Jody took her
piece reluctantly as if she thought it might bite her.
But Dill was wolfing his down hungrily, so at last
she broke off a bit and chewed it. It didn't taste too
good, it was a little flat and not as sweet as it should
have been. And the nuts weren't properly crunchy.
But Dill didn't seem to mind. While Jody watched
he cut another slice. In twenty minutes he'd eaten
nearly the whole cake.

"I keep hoping the next piece will taste better,"
he told Jody. "Next time think more about how

the thing's going to taste and less about how it looks, will you?" He scraped up some icing with one finger and swallowed it thoughtfully. "Not near enough orange juice."

Jody looked at him anxiously. "How do you feel?" she asked.

"Pretty terrible," he answered, holding his stomach. "Like I'd eaten a magazine." He took one more bite and then picked up the plate. "Now, listen, Jody, one thing's for sure, we don't want Mother and Daddy to know about this. It can be about the neatest thing that ever happened to us, but you know how grownups are. They'd take you to a doctor and get you cured or something. So we got to be careful. I'm going to hide what's left of this cake and the plate, and you go wash the saucers and knife. Don't let Mother see you."

He opened the screen door and gave a furtive look around the house before he scurried away. Jody picked up the saucers and went into the kitchen. She set one of them down on the sink. She frowned at it a moment.

"Be a bowl of goldfish," she ordered, and there it was, a round crystal bowl with two tiny flashing fishes in it, and a long strand of green milfoil. Jody touched the bowl timidly. It felt quite solid and real. And the water was thoroughly wet.

"Be the saucer again," she said, and there was the

little flowered bowl sitting on the wooden drain-
board. Jody felt dizzy with excitement and impor-
tance. It really was magic or something. She could
sort of work miracles!

She couldn't help grinning a little. Horrible Dill
had better watch his step.

Chapter Three

"Now the thing to do," explained Dill, "is to find out just what you can do and what you can't. Then we'll make a list of things we want. And we'll go around the house and collect—"

"We!" said Jody calmly. "I'm the one who can do this, Dill Tracy. And I don't want to make out any list."

"Aw, Jody, don't be a crumb," cried Dill. "I wouldn't leave you out if it was me that could do it. What are you—a pig or something?"

Jody relented. She felt sure Dill wouldn't leave her out. He might make her life miserable by teasing and tormenting, but he wouldn't leave her out of anything.

"Oh, all right," she said at last. "I wasn't going to leave you out, anyway. It wouldn't be much fun by myself, I guess. But, Dill, listen. If I get you all those things you want, you have to promise to quit being mean."

"Sure, I promise," said Dill amiably, without having the least idea what she was talking about.

"You have to stop pulling my hair and calling me Goggle-eyes," Jody went on relentlessly, "and don't splash me when we go swimming or push me in when I'm standing on the side. And don't hide in the hall and jump at me."

"Oh, rats, Jody," cried Dill. "That isn't being mean. That's just being friendly."

"Well, I think it's being mean," Jody answered. "And you have to stop."

"Okay, okay," agreed Dill. "I'll try, anyway." He picked up a rock and held it out to her. "Now change this into something."

Jody hesitated. "No," she said finally. "I made you into a squirrel, and I made a cake for you. Now I'm going to do something for me. You never know when this might wear off or something."

"Gee, do you think so?" asked Dill. "What a disappointment."

"Well, it just might," she answered. "Now, hush." She picked up a leaf and looked hard at it. Because of changing the saucer into the bowl of goldfish, she knew it was easy enough to do this. All she had to do was picture what she wanted in her mind, and as soon as she said the words, why, there it was.

But there wasn't any point in letting Dill know this. He might as well be impressed with how hard it was. So she screwed up her face and held her breath and squirmed around and tried to look as though she was exerting a tremendous effort.

"Be a chocolate sundae," she said at last.

And in her hand instead of the leaf's faintly scratchy touch was the weight of something cold and hard, a glass dish heaped with ice cream, with shiny brown chocolate sauce sliding down the white slopes. On the very top was a cherry, and a spoon stuck out from the side of the dish. It looked simply wonderful.

"Gosh, is that all you could do?" asked Dill scornfully. "I thought you were going to end up with a roast turkey."

"It's what I wanted," said Jody, eying it hungrily.

"Is things to eat all you can manage?" Dill wanted to know.

"I turned you into a squirrel," Jody retorted indignantly.

"Lots of people eat squirrels," Dill told her. "I bet things to eat *is* all you can do."

"No, it isn't," protested Jody.

"Well, prove it," Dill said, holding out his rock

again. "No, wait. Let's eat the sundae first, before it melts."

He reached for the spoon, but Jody suddenly grabbed his arm. "No, don't!" she cried.

"Well, for Pete's sake, why not?" he asked.

"I just thought, that leaf might have been poisonous," Jody explained. "You know how, after you ate the cake you said you felt like you'd eaten a magazine? If you ate the sundae, you might feel like you'd eaten a poisonous leaf."

He gave her an admiring look. "Gee, Jody, you're positively dangerous," he said. "Well, never mind, next time we have applesauce or Jello for dessert you can turn it into a sundae. Now do this rock."

"What'll I change it into?" she asked.

Dill pondered. "A magnifying glass," he said at last. "A big one."

Jody concentrated. "Be a magnifying glass," she said to the rock. And there it was, a fine, big glass with a metal rim and a black handle.

"Neat!" cried Dill. "Gee, thanks, Jody. Hey, looky this ant. He looks big as a dog."

They spent some time peering at ants and leaves, the inside of half a robin's egg they found under a tree, some moss, and a rhododendron blossom. Dill showed Jody how the glass would gather and converge the rays of the sun and make the damp leaves crisp and curl and smoke.

"Don't leave it smoldering," warned Jody. "That's the way forest fires start."

"Do you think I'm dumb or something?" asked Dill, grinding the leaves under his foot. "I've spent enough summers up here to know about fires and being careful. Anyway, we don't have to worry this time of year. The woods are still dripping from all that rain last month."

But to show Jody he knew about such things, he buried the leaves under a handful of earth.

They were still looking at a grasshopper's leg when Aunt Margaret called them to lunch. "Aw, heck," said Dill. "I planned on having a motorbike and a hunting knife and a record player by lunch time. I bet Mother'll want me to go into Wolf Town with her this afternoon. I bet we never get a chance to do anything good. Come on back out here as soon as you can, will you, Jody?"

He was right, and Aunt Margaret did want him to go into Wolf Town with her. As a matter of fact, Jody went too, to help with the week's grocery shopping and some other errands. So it was after supper before she and Dill managed any privacy.

In Dill's room they sat side by side on the edge of Dill's bottom bunk bed. They had to sit on the very edge because of all the things on it, all the things Dill meant to put away some time, like his chess set and the pair of blue jeans that were only a little

muddy and could probably be worn again if his
mother didn't look at him too closely; and the
things that he couldn't make up his mind what to
do with, like a gourd dipper with a leak in it and a
rock that might have fossils in it and three or four
comic books that he had read once but might want
to read again; and the things that he didn't exactly have a place for, like his tennis racket and a
coconut that his grandmother had sent him from
Florida, and the insides of an electric clock.

He slept on the top bunk, so there were only a
few books and a baseball bat up there.

"Can you still do it?" he asked Jody as soon as
they had managed to squeeze in among all these
things.

"I guess so," she answered. She picked up a comic
book and held it out in front of her.

"Be careful," cried Dill. "Don't waste yourself.
You might run down like a battery. Turn it into
something we really want, like a motorbike."

"What are you going to tell your mother when a
motorbike turns up in your bedroom?" Jody wanted
to know.

"Gee, that's right," he said and scratched his head.
"I couldn't say I found it, could I?" He thought a
minute. "We'll just have to think of some good explanation before we do it. Say, how about money?

Can you turn that comic book into money? So I could buy a motorbike?"

Aunt Margaret's big yellow cat Tamsine jumped up on Jody's lap and began to push his head against her arm and purr loudly. Jody concentrated on the comic book. "Be a five-dollar bill," she said slowly.

The bill was new and crisp. Jody turned it over and over. It looked all right. But somehow she was uneasy. As she well knew, money and magic didn't mix. People who wished for wealth always ended up with puddings stuck to their noses, or even worse misfortunes.

And Dill might call it science, but she still thought it was magic.

"Here," Dill said, thrusting the rest of the comic books into her lap where Tamsine promptly lay down on them. "And don't bother with five-dollar bills. Twenties or hundreds will do just fine."

Jody stroked Tamsine, who rolled over on his back and purred in a loud high giggle.

"No," she said finally, "I don't think I'd better. It wouldn't be honest somehow. And besides, Dill, it isn't going to be a bit easier to explain how you got three or four hundred dollars than it would be to explain how you got a motorbike."

"Sure it would," cried Dill. "I could say I was out in the woods and stopped a runaway horse with a little girl on it and saved her life and her father was a millionaire and he gave me the money for a reward."

"Well, you could say that," said Jody scornfully. "But it would be a big fat lie and it certainly sounds like one. I can just hear what Aunt Margaret and Uncle John would say."

"Maybe we could find the money somewhere," Dill went on. "We could be digging a hole down by the creek and find a chest full of money left by pirates. Or maybe bank robbers. I guess there wouldn't be any pirates up here in the mountains."

"If bank robbers left it, it would have to go back to the bank," Jody pointed out. "Anyway, Daddy told me if you dug up something like that—money or treasure or anything—you had to give it to the government if you couldn't find the rightful owner."

Dill looked despairing. "I guess you'll have to stick to things to eat," he said gloomily. "That way we can destroy the evidence. They'd find out about anything else."

Working miracles did have its problems that Jody hadn't considered.

"Of course, we could go way out in the woods and I could turn a stick into a motorbike for you and you could ride it there," said Jody slowly. Dill, who was always one to consider half a loaf better than none, brightened considerably.

"Yeah," he cried. "And when I got through riding it you could turn it back into a stick and we wouldn't even have to try to hide it."

That wouldn't be as much fun as riding it around where everybody could see it. He'd counted on taking it home with him and showing off a little. He'd be the only boy in his grade who had a motorbike. He'd sort of planned on riding it to school. But this way was better than nothing.

We can do that tomorrow, Jody thought. But I wish there was something we could do now.

She wondered if chocolate fudge made out of a comic book would be as fattening as chocolate fudge made out of sugar and butter and cocoa? She pushed Tamsine off her lap and picked up one of the comic books.

But she supposed it would be fattening. And anyway she'd just finished supper, so she wasn't really hungry. Tamsine rubbed against her ankles and looked up to see what had made her shove him out of his comfortable place. What beautiful eyes he had, greenish with gold fires in them, like a tiger's.

"Be a tiger, Tamsine," said Jody, almost without thinking.

Jody didn't know how Dill managed to get up on the top bunk bed so fast, but she knew he was there because when she drew back from Tamsine her head hit the bulge where his weight made the

mattress sag. She was too terrified to say anything, however. She just squeezed slowly back between the coconut and the gourd dipper, and stared, fascinated, at Tamsine.

Tamsine made a magnificent tiger. Under his thick striped coat his muscles ebbed and flowed. His tawny eyes glowed in his flat broad head and his huge white fangs showed when he lifted his black lip.

Except for the tiger's rasping purr, there was silence in Dill's room. Jody opened her mouth to say, "Be Tamsine," but nothing came out except a tiny, tiny squeak.

And anyway she had forgotten what Tamsine looked like. The tiger filled her mind as he seemed to fill the room, with flashing gold and black and gleam of slashing teeth.

"Margaret," shouted Uncle John, "have you seen that *Quarterly* I left out on the side porch?"

The tiger turned his wide head toward the door. His eyes slitted into two green crescents. "Turn him back, Jody," whispered Dill frantically. "Turn him back!"

Tamsine uttered a loud purr and stretched his neck trying to see Dill. Then he stood up and put his huge front paws on the top bunk. Jody could see his creamy underside and the way his long lovely tail wound between his legs. His fur brushed her knees.

The bulge in the mattress moved swiftly toward the wall. Uncle John's footsteps sounded on the stairs. "Margaret," he called, "are you up there?"

"For Pete's sake, Jody!" Dill's low voice was agonized. "What's the matter with you? He's going to eat me!"

Jody swallowed hard. She was trying for all she was worth. But somehow she couldn't make her jaws move. She couldn't say the words. Her whole works seemed paralyzed, as she told Dill later. She was so scared she could hardly breathe.

"Margaret," said Uncle John, right outside the door.

"Jody!" squealed Dill.

"Purra-wurra," said the tiger.

Chapter Four

"Tamsine!" gasped Jody hoarsely. "Be Tamsine!"

Uncle John poked his head in the door. "Do you know where your Aunt Margaret is?" he asked Jody.

Jody stared at him silently. Her heart was pounding in her chest. Dill came suddenly rolling down off the top bunk.

"Yes, sir, she said she might go over to the Rabuns' for a few minutes. And I heard the car a little while ago, so I guess she's left," he said. Tamsine wound slowly in and out between his feet.

"Oh," said Uncle John. "I'd forgotten that. I took a walk down by the creek and I didn't hear her leave." He glanced down at Tamsine. "Funny thing, when I was coming up the steps I could see Tamsine's shadow on the wall in the hall. He looked as big as a tiger. Some trick of the light, I suppose."

He went out and they could hear him going downstairs.

"Some trick is right," hissed Dill. "Jody, what got into you?"

"I was scared," confessed Jody.

"I was scared too," said Dill. "Whatever made you do it? Suppose Dad had seen that tiger? Or worse yet, suppose Tamsine had clawed my arm off?"

"Oh, do you really think Tamsine would have hurt you?" cried Jody.

"Tamsine might not have, but that tiger sure would," Dill told her. "You ought to see the rips he made in my sheets and mattress."

"Oh, dear," said Jody, "how'll you explain that to Aunt Margaret?"

"It won't matter. All the things in this house are pretty old and raggedy anyway," Dill explained cheerfully. "And I guess Mother's not surprised at anything that happens to my sheets. At least she never has said anything, not even the time Bill Rabun and I used one to carry a snapping turtle around in."

Poor Aunt Margaret, she really does have a hard time, thought Jody.

"Anyway, you'd better think twice before you do something like that," Dill warned. "It was kind of fun; Tamsine made a neat tiger. But, wow! What a pickle we'd have been in if Dad had seen him!"

Jody gave Tamsine a timid look. She didn't know whether or not she wanted him to sleep on her window sill any more.

"Come on," urged Dill. "Let's go outside and turn a stick into a motorbike."

"Stupid, it's getting dark outside," said Jody. "You couldn't see to ride."

"Sure, a motorbike has lights, like a car," said Dill.

"Well, I think it's your turn to think twice," said Jody. "You'd have to walk miles and miles out into the woods to get to a place where nobody could see you or hear you. You know how dark and still it is up here at nights."

"Oh, rats," complained Dill. "I guess you're right. But let's do it first thing in the morning, hear, Jody? Please?"

"Okay," agreed Jody, and she yawned. "Right now I better go write Mother a letter. I meant to do it yesterday and then all this happened."

Back in her room Jody sat at the unsteady little table by her bed and opened a box of letter paper. Aunt Margaret had given it to her. It was just plain white paper without anything on it. At home Jody had a box of letter paper with a bunch of little pink roses in the corner of every sheet, and another box with kittens all across the tops of the sheets and on

the inside of the envelopes, but she had forgotten
to bring it. So she had to use this plain old white
paper, and it looked so dull and empty. It was hard
to fill up a page without putting in some complaints
about Dill or how lonesome she was or not getting
to go to the beach. She tried to be cheerful, but before she got through something dismal crept into
every letter.

Now, of course, she had plenty to fill up this
page. But she didn't dare tell it.

Oh, if she could only work a miracle on this summer and make it be the kind of summer it had
started out to be!

She picked up a sheet of paper and stared at it.

"Be a five-dollar bill," she whispered.

The money crackled in her fingers. If she could
only turn this paper into enough money to pay for
college for Steve and Roger! Then Daddy could
come home from France, and Steve and Roger
could quit their jobs, and they could all go to the
seashore together.

She turned the bill over and over. What a funny
thing money was! Just a piece of paper, she thought,
but having it when you needed it could make a lot
of difference. Daddy had explained it to her once,
how this paper wasn't really worth anything, but
stood for silver and gold kept in the Treasury, or
something like that.

Of course, since she had made this money, there wouldn't be any silver or gold for this bill.

It was counterfeit then! That was what had made her feel uneasy about the bill she had made for Dill. It was counterfeit, and it was cheating to use it. And besides, she might have to go to jail for making it. Jody was quite certain she didn't want to go to jail, not even in order to buy Daddy an extra-special birthday present.

She sighed and ordered the bill to become a sheet of letter paper again. But after a minute she turned the plain white sheet into a sheet of palest green, with a spray of delicate white flowers in the corner. That wasn't counterfeiting, and it was a pleasure to write on.

"Dear Mother," she began.

"Here's a good spot," said Dill. "It's miles from any place, and nobody can hear. The ground's fairly level and there aren't too many trees, so I can do some real riding."

Jody nodded. Dill was so pleased and excited about the motorbike, she was beginning to be a little excited herself. She really did owe him something. He was keeping his part of the bargain and hardly teased her at all. As a matter of fact, she kind of missed it. Life was pretty dull without Dill's teasing.

Now she got a stick from among some blackberry bushes and laid it on the ground in front of them. She stared at it a moment and then she glanced at Dill.

"Well, go on," he cried. "What's the matter? What's stopping you?"

Jody looked foolish. "I can't do it," she said finally. "I don't know what a motorbike looks like."

"Oh, good grief, sure you do," cried Dill. "Roger had one, remember? He used to let you and me take turns doubling with him."

"That was years ago," Jody pointed out. "I was hardly even eight. I can barely remember it."

"Well, try hard," urged Dill desperately. "A motorbike's just about like a bike except it's bigger and heavier and has a motor. Roger's was red, remember?"

Jody screwed up her face tight with the effort of remembering. She pointed at the stick and said, "Be a motorbike!"

The machine was red, anyway, and shiny and new-looking. Dill walked slowly around it. He shook his head. "I think this is more like a motorcycle than a motorbike. I don't know whether I can manage it or not," he said.

"Well, it's the best I can do," said Jody, stroking the bright fenders. "If I could see one again, maybe I could do a better job."

Dill mounted the seat and stretched his legs to reach the footrests. "Are you sure you weren't thinking about a motorcycle?" he asked. "A motorbike has pedals, and this doesn't."

He punched some buttons, and the lights came on. "See, it's got a starter, like a motorcycle." He kicked at something near his foot, and the engine whirred and coughed and died. The machine shuddered from one end to the other.

"Well, anyway, it works," he said delightedly. "I don't know how you can make an engine that works when you can't make a motorbike that isn't about two thirds motorcycle."

He squeezed and turned the interesting little gadgets on the handle bars.

"Look here, Jody," he began, turning toward her. As he moved, his foot struck the starter once again. With a sudden roar the vehicle leaped into life and careened through the bushes.

"Be careful, Dill," cried Jody as the motorbike-motorcycle whizzed straight at a tree and then at the last moment veered aside. "Oh, look out!"

Wobbling and wavering, Dill sped in and out among the oaks and hickories. He was going faster and faster, and Jody thought he looked a little scared as he rushed by her, clinging to the handle bars.

"Oh, watch out!" she shrieked as he vanished

down a steep slope. She ran to look down after him,
but just as she reached the top of the hill he came
roaring back up, straight at her. Jody screamed and
jumped backward, tripped, and fell full length
among the blackberry bushes. The motorbike turned
sharply and desperately to one side and crashed

smack into a tree. From among the briers Jody heard the clatter of the falling machine and the engine's last faint growls and groans. She struggled up, sobbing, and ran toward Dill, who lay stretched at the foot of the tree, still as a stone.

"Oh, Dill!" she wept. "Are you hurt? Are you dead?"

After a minute Dill sat up and rubbed his arm and untangled part of the handle bars from around his left ankle.

"I don't think I'm old enough to drive one of these things," he said at last. "I bet it isn't legal."

Jody sighed with relief. He wasn't dead. He didn't even appear to be broken anywhere. Of course, he was bruised and scratched, but Aunt Margaret was used to that. Jody was pretty much scratched and bumped herself.

"And I've lost my glasses," she said crossly. "Get up, Dill, and help me look."

But Dill was busy examining a gash in one knee and a big black-and-blue spot on one of his arms. "I think I broke a rib," he said, poking himself in the chest. Jody went over and rummaged among the blackberry runners until she found the glasses. They weren't broken, but one ear piece was badly bent.

Dill got up and set off toward home, limping and holding his hand against his ribs. Jody put on the glasses, with the bent ear piece sticking out from her head at a wild angle, and started after him. She'd only gone a few steps when she remembered the motorbike. She ran back and pointed an accusing finger at the tangled mass of red metal and wheels. "Be a stick," she said severely.

What an ordinary-looking little dry branch, to have caused so much commotion, she thought as she ran to catch up with Dill.

At lunch Aunt Margaret listened to a very complicated explanation of the accident. It wasn't lying, Jody thought, as Dill talked on and on, but it wasn't exactly the truth. They *couldn't* tell Aunt Margaret the truth, as Dill pointed out; she wouldn't believe it.

"All I can say," Mrs. Tracy declared finally, "is that I never suspected there were so many fierce trees running around in the woods waiting for an opportunity to attack innocent children."

"Could I have another sandwich, please?" asked Dill.

Aunt Margaret passed the sandwiches. "At least this accident hasn't seemed to affect your appetites," she said dryly. Jody shot her an indignant look. She'd only eaten one sandwich. The truth was Dill smelled so horribly of various ointments and liniments, he took her appetite away.

"Jody, I have to go to Wolf Town this afternoon," Aunt Margaret said. "There's a man in the bank there who will mend that ear piece. When I get ready to leave, remind me to take your glasses."

"Yes'm," said Jody meekly.

"Now," Aunt Margaret went on, "today is Thursday. So while I'm gone, you know what has to be done."

"Yes'm," said Jody again. Dill groaned. On Thursdays Dill and Jody were supposed to clean their rooms. They put clean sheets on their beds, picked up clothes and books, tidied table tops, and ran a desultory dust mop under beds and chairs. Jody didn't mind. It wasn't half as much work as cleaning her room at home. But Dill always acted as if he'd been asked to perform all Hercules' twelve labors, his father said.

"There are popsicles in the freezer if you want them," Aunt Margaret said as she stood up. "The clean sheets are on the table in the upstairs hall, and the dust mops are in the closet in the kitchen. There are three of them, so I think Dill ought to be able to find one if he looks." Dill's usual excuse for not mopping the floor was that he couldn't find a mop.

"All right, I'll do it right away," he said calmly. Aunt Margaret and Jody both looked at him suspiciously. He was up to something, Jody was sure. He had a glint in his eye. But he didn't say anything more. He just limped out into the kitchen and got himself a banana popsicle. Jody took an orange one and went outside with it, where she wouldn't have to smell the mingled odors of banana and liniment.

When she'd finished, she fetched a dust mop from the closet and carried it up to her room. Dill was sitting on her bed, holding his clean sheets in his arms. He was grinning quietly to himself.

"What do you want?" asked Jody. "You better go make your bed."

"Listen," exclaimed Dill. "How would you like never to have to make a bed again? How would you like to be free from worry and care forever?"

Jody giggled. "You sound like a TV commercial," she said. "What are you talking about?"

Dill sprang up and then groaned and held his ribs. "Ouch," he yelped. "Jody, I just can't make my bed today. So you can have it done for me, see? You can make me a bedmaker! All you have to do is say the word."

Jody stared. "You mean a robot?" she asked in a whisper.

Dill considered. "No," he said at last. "I've seen robots, and they're not so hot. They really can't do much. And the mixed-up way you do things, you'd probably end up with something that wouldn't work at all. I was thinking about something alive that could move around and work and think and take orders. Sort of like 'The Sorcerer's Apprentice.' "

Miss Osborne, Jody's fourth-grade teacher, had told her class the story of the sorcerer's small apprentice and had played the music that went with it. Jody remembered it well, so now she hesitated. "But he got in all kinds of trouble," she reminded Dill.

"Yes, but that was because he was messing around with someone else's magic," Dill pointed out. "This is all yours—and I don't think it's magic, anyhow. Try it, Jody. If you don't like it, you can always turn it back."

He seized the dust mop and turned it upside down.

"Here, use this," he said. "But be careful. Make
sure it has all the things it needs, like eyes and ears
and hands."

Jody gazed at the mop. It would be kind of fun.
And as Dill said, she could undo it when she wanted
to. "Be alive," she said slowly. "With arms and legs
and ears and eyes, and a mouth and a brain."

She must have been thinking about Miss Osborne.
Certainly the creature which stood before her now
was thinner and grayer than Miss Osborne, but not
much. Its fluffy hair fell over its face just as Miss
Osborne's did. And when it spoke it spoke in Miss
Osborne's high fluty elegant voice. "What a lovely
day," it said, which was exactly what Miss Osborne
said every morning, even if a blizzard was raging
outside.

Dill chortled. "Boy, oh, boy, this is neat," he
cried.

"Jody," called Aunt Margaret. "I'm leaving now.
Would you bring me your glasses?"

Jody took off her glasses and ran out into the
hall. Aunt Margaret was standing at the top of the
stairs. "Thanks, Aunt Margaret," said Jody.

"No trouble," said Aunt Margaret. "You and
Dill work hard. I want your rooms to look extra nice
because Uncle John's bringing home company tomorrow. So make your beds neatly and mop
thoroughly."

"All right," agreed Jody, smiling, and she ran back into her room. Dill was walking gleefully around Miss Osborne-the-Mop.

"It's very impolite to stare," said the Mop sharply. Dill paid no attention. He picked up his clean sheets and pillowcases from Jody's bed.

"Here," he ordered. "Go into my room and make up my bed."

The Mop drew itself up stiffly. From behind its woolly gray hair its eyes suddenly gleamed out. It certainly *was* like Miss Osborne, Jody thought. That was exactly the way she looked when the class got noisy and badly behaved.

"Don't be rude, young man," said the Mop. "I have no intention of doing your work for you. I heard your mother say you were to do a thorough job on your room. And I think you'd better get at it."

Dill glared at the Mop, and it glared back. After a minute Dill's eyes dropped. He turned and went out, carrying the sheets, and Jody heard him in his room pulling his bed out from the wall, getting ready to put on the clean sheets.

Chapter Five

"I expect you had better get busy too," the Mop said briskly to Jody.

"I—um, yes," responded Jody, and began to strip the sheets from her bed. On her skinny little legs the Mop moved over to the window and looked out. She hummed a tuneless little hum. Just like Miss Osborne, thought Jody.

"A lovely day," murmured the Mop. "A really lovely day."

Jody worked extra carefully to please Aunt Margaret. She really rather liked to make up a bed. She snapped the fresh-smelling clean sheet so that it belled up and then floated slowly down to settle over the mattress. She was folding the blanket when Dill came clattering into the room.

"What's that still doing here?" he demanded, pointing an accusing finger at the Mop. The Mop gave him a haughty look.

Jody was startled. She had forgotten that she would have to turn the Mop back into an ordinary dust mop. As a matter of fact, she had come to think of the Mop as Miss Osborne almost altogether. And, of course, turning Miss Osborne into a dust mop would take a good deal of courage as well as magical powers.

"Come on, Jody," urged Dill. "I need the mop. Turn it back into a mop."

"Oh, well, all right," mumbled Jody. "But she wasn't hurting anything, just looking out the window."

"She wasn't *doing* anything either," Dill pointed out. "If she isn't going to be a help, she'll have to be turned back. Jody, you really fouled that one up. Make her be a mop again and then fix us something that will really work. You can do it if you go at it the right way, I know you can. Not that it'll do me any good," he added sourly. "I already made my bed."

Jody placed the folded blanket on her bed. She didn't look in the Mop's direction. It was sort of horrible to think about turning her back into a dust mop when she was sitting there so happily enjoying the sunshine.

"See, what you do this time," Dill went on, "is tell the Mop it *has* to obey orders and do exactly what it's told. Get a move on, Jody. We want to get everything done before Mother gets back."

Jody slid her eyes toward the Mop. "Don't talk so loud," she whispered. Dill looked surprised. "Why not?" he asked. "It's just a dust mop, and a pretty crumby one at that!"

"Well, I can't help thinking she has feelings," Jody admitted. "And she seems kind of nice, in a way, sort of."

Dill was scornful. "She's a crumby dust mop," he said firmly. "And you got to get rid of her, Jody, you know you got to. You can't let her keep on hanging out the window that way. Suppose somebody saw her."

"Oh, I guess you're right," said Jody. She walked very quietly up to the Mop and leveled a finger at her. "Be a dust mop again," she said softly.

The Mop continued to gaze out the window. "Be a dust mop," repeated Jody. The Mop turned and looked at her. "You're a very rude child," she said witheringly.

Dill clutched Jody's arm. "You're not trying," he cried. "Come on, Jody. I need that mop. Concentrate, hear?"

A little cold finger of fear ran up and down Jody's spine. She *had* been concentrating, she knew

she had. Was something wrong? She drew a deep
breath and fastened her eyes steadily on the top
of the Mop's head, where it was easy enough to vis-
ualize her as really a dust mop. "Be the dust mop,"
Jody said once more, keeping her voice firm.

"Really!" the Mop declared in tones of outrage.
"I have never been so insulted in my life. I shall
have to tell your aunt about this. I am quite certain
she would want to know how badly you've been be-
having."

Dill groaned. "Jody, did you really try?" Jody
glared at him. Then she turned once more to the
Mop. "Be a dust mop, be a dust mop, be a dust mop,"
she chanted rapidly. She was concentrating so hard
it made her dizzy and she had to shut her eyes for
a second. When she opened them again, the Mop
was flouncing across the room.

"Oh, golly, it's happened," said Dill. "You've run
down. And you couldn't have picked a worse time."

"Well, it wasn't my fault," Jody exclaimed indignantly. "Who wanted a live dust mop anyway? I
didn't mind cleaning my room. It isn't much work
and I never wanted any old dust mop running
around doing it for me—" she broke off and fumbled
for a piece of Kleenex in the pocket of her shorts.

"Don't cry, for pity's sake," whispered Dill. "Gosh,
Jody, don't cry. This is a life-or-death emergency,
and we haven't got time for crying. Mother'll be

back in an hour and when she gets back . . . *what are we going to do with that mop?"*

Jody wrung her hands. "Oh, I don't know!" she cried. "Oh, how awful! What can anybody do with a live dust mop?"

"Well, we better calm down and think what to do," said Dill. He turned around and looked at the Mop, who was leaning against a chair, looking scandalized. He wondered if she could sit down. She seemed to bend in very awkward places. "I guess the first thing to do is lock her in a closet or something."

Jody too looked at the Mop. "Oh, Dill, that would be cruel. And anyway she'd just yell her head off—or her mop off, or whatever you call it." She paused, thinking. "I guess the best thing would be to try to make up with her. Be very nice to her, and maybe she'll be quiet till we can smuggle her out of the house."

"It seems like she'd be right at home in a closet," said Dill. "But maybe you're right. Go tell her you're sorry."

Jody started to argue and point out that she wasn't the one who had been rude to the Mop in the first place. But then she changed her mind. There wasn't time to argue, and anyway she really was sorry.

She looked at the Mop rather timidly. She'd always been just a tiny bit scared of Miss Osborne,

and the Mop was very like Miss Osborne. "Oh, Miss
Os—Miss Mop, I mean," Jody began, in as polite
a voice as she could manage in spite of the fact that
it was a little unsteady. "We . . . we want to apologize.
We didn't mean to hurt your feelings. It was just
a game, a—a sort of joke. We didn't mean it and
we're sorry."

The Mop turned her head and stared out the
window as if she hadn't heard. But after a minute
she answered faintly, "It was very rude. It gave me
quite a shock." She put one of her skinny hands to
her head and sighed deeply. "But you've apologized
very nicely," she went on, suddenly brisk. "I'm sure
you'll be more considerate in the future. I forgive
you both. And now I think you'd better hurry and
get these rooms tidy. I'm sure you're both eager to
please Mrs. Whatever-her-name-is, your aunt, Jody.
I sincerely hope that you intend to have this room
completely cleaned by the time she gets back." She
switched her gaze to Dill. "And you too, young
man," she added severely.

Dill gave Jody a baleful glance and stalked out of
the room. Jody went silently back to work. She put
all her books back into the little bookcase, tidied
the top of her table and dresser, and then went down
to the kitchen and got a second dust mop. She looked
at it thoughtfully. Who would have thought such
an innocent-looking piece of equipment could lead

you into such a mess? Because they *were* in a mess, she told herself as she went back up the stairs. There just wasn't any way you could tell a grown person that you had made a dust mop come alive and now you couldn't undo it.

And what in the world were they going to do with this Mop? Especially with company coming, they couldn't leave her to run around the house, like the Old Form in the tale of Titty Mouse and Tatty Mouse. She frowned as she pushed the second mop back and forth over the worn boards of the floor.

She took the mop into Dill's room, leaving Miss Osborne-the-Mop still gazing dreamily out of the window.

"What are we going to do?" she asked Dill in a whisper.

"We'll have to get her outside," he answered. Jody looked gloomy. That part would be easy. The Mop had already told her three times how much she loved the outdoors. "I mean after that?" she asked.

Dill pondered. "We'll take her down to the creek and push her in," he said grimly.

Jody's eyes flew wide. "But that's murder!" she cried. "Dill, we couldn't!"

"Jody, do you want to spend the rest of your life trying to keep up with a live dust mop?" Dill wanted to know. "It wouldn't be murder anyway. She's not a person, she's just a dusty old dust mop." He frowned. "I don't guess I really could do it. Anyway, she wouldn't drown, she'd float. She'd end up in Wolf Town, probably. The creek goes right through it. And can't you see what would happen in Wolf Town if a mop floated by Main Street hollering for help." He grinned a little, but Jody didn't think it was funny.

They finished Dill's room, working together. It really looked very nice when they got through. They arranged the spread on his bottom bunk bed so that it hung down to the floor and nobody could see the coconut and the disemboweled electric clock and the other things they had shoved under there for lack of any other place to put them.

"I'll go get her," said Jody, glancing uneasily toward her own room. "I'll tell her we want to show her the scenery down by the creek. At least she'll be out of the house when Aunt Margaret gets back."

Dill seized her arm. "Just a minute, Jody," he said. He held out an old comic book. Dill seemed to have barrels of comic books, Jody thought. She wondered where in the world he got them all.

"Try one more time," he went on. "See if you can't do it. Change this into a cookie. With nuts in it." And then he hastily snatched the magazine away. "No, don't. Suppose you could do it just one more time and you wasted it on a cookie! When we get down to the creek, I'll hold the Mop's attention somehow and you try once more on her. And try *hard*."

Jody nodded. She rummaged around in her brain a little bit to see if she could tell what had happened to make her lose her power, but she couldn't think of anything. She hadn't changed a bit, as far as she knew. She felt the same as always, like Joan Ransom, aged eleven and too fat.

It was easy to persuade the Mop to come outside.

"The world of the outdoors is so truly beautiful and inspiring," she cried as she stubbed across the porch and down the steps.

"Yes, isn't it?" agreed Dill. He was being ferociously polite, holding open doors and helping her down the steps. "The rhododendron is in bloom down by the creek. We'll show you."

The Mop paused by a big clump of yellow lilies and gave a little admiring cry.

Jody sniffed. "They smell so sweet," she said.

The Mop looked confused. "What? What?" she exclaimed.

Jody glanced at her curiously. I guess she can't smell, she thought. That was one thing I forgot to mention when I invented her or whatever it was.

"Come along," said Dill impatiently, almost forgetting to be polite. He was afraid his mother would come home and find him walking down the path with a live dust mop. "Hurry, it's much prettier down by the creek."

But the Mop was not to be hurried. She meandered along, commenting on how blue the sky was and how white the clouds. When at last they had put the first bend of the path between them and the house, Dill wiped his brow and said, "Whew!" Now, even if his mother came home, she couldn't see them.

It was shady and cool along the path. Underfoot, even under the Mop's curious little wooden-looking feet, the thick layer of brown needles from the pines and balsams and hemlocks muffled the sound of their steps. The wind barely whispered overhead. And suddenly quite close a bird began to sing, the same song Jody had heard before by the creek. Through the shadows came that clear sweet voice, seeming to twine in upon itself and spin down into silence before it began again.

"Listen," murmured Jody. The Mop halted, her head tilted. Jody watched her closely. Miss Osborne had known a lot about birds, she remembered. Maybe the Mop had sort of inherited her knowledge. Maybe she could tell what the name of the singer was.

"What is it?" asked Jody softly. "What's singing?"

"It's the voice of the fruit-frosted cupcake," answered the Mop firmly. Jody's mouth dropped open. Dill put his hand over his mouth to hide his grin.

When the Mop trotted off the path to get a closer look at some mushrooms, he nudged Jody. "What'd you expect?" he asked. "Raised in a broom closet!"

When at last they reached the creek, the children were worn out with exclaiming and admiring, and glad to sit watching the water sliding eternally over its little falls and booming in among the rocks. The Mop sat beside them, still marveling.

Finally Dill gave Jody another punch. She wished he wouldn't; her ribs were getting as black and blue as his. "What'll we do now?" he asked softly. "We can stay out here this afternoon, but sooner or later we'll have to go home."

Jody shook her head glumly. "It's rude to whisper," said the Mop reprovingly.

"I'm sorry," apologized Dill. "You seemed to be enjoying the peace and quiet. I didn't want to interrupt you."

"Oh," said the Mop in mollified tones. "Well, it really is most pleasant here. I believe I could stay here forever."

Dill brightened. "It's a wonderful place," he agreed. "It's especially nice at night. The—the artificial flavoring is in bloom and it attracts thousands of lightning bugs. And—and you can hear the fly-by-nights singing. Lots of people spend the night here just for their singing."

"Fly-by-nights!" cried the Mop. "It must really

be most exciting. I should love to hear them. And
see them, too, if it could be arranged."

Dill jumped up. "Oh, that's easy," he told her.
"I know a place where you can spend the night. I've
often done it myself, and some other people have
stayed there too. It's a fine place."

The Mop clasped her skinny little hands. "How
thrilling!" she exclaimed. "Is it close by?"

Jody knew what Dill was talking about. There
was a little cave farther up the creek where he and
Bill Rabun sometimes camped out. They had some
blankets and cooking things there. It would be a
fine place to hide the Mop. But would she be willing
to stay there? Jody didn't think so. It was so spidery
and dim in the cave, she didn't like to stay there
herself, not even in daylight.

But she underestimated Dill. There was a stump
outside the cave, a big tall smooth-topped stump.

"Sit here," said Dill, helping the Mop up on the
stump, where she sat very awkwardly indeed, like
some kind of enormous insect. It was going to be
hard for her to get down, Jody thought.

"Now," Dill went on, "you get a good view from
here. And when you want to go to bed, there's a
bed right inside the . . . the doorway there." He
waved a hand in the direction of the cave. The
Mop twisted her head around. She couldn't see

much of the cave, and Jody knew she wasn't going
to climb off that stump and back on again.

"Oh, yes, a bed," she said vaguely. She was still
murmuring about fly-by-nights when Jody and Dill
left her, explaining that they had to go home to
supper.

"I bet she's mad when she sees that bed," Jody
told Dill as they went back up the path. "Do you
suppose she eats? And if she does eat, what does
she like?"

"Hay," said Dill. "Hay and ham sandwiches. I
don't guess she eats. It's like being able to smell.
You never mentioned it when you brought her alive.
And maybe she won't like the bed, but can you
think of anything else to do with her?"

But neither of them mentioned the real worry—
what to do with the Mop tomorrow.

When Jody woke the next day, she knew it was
early. The sky had the look, misty and exciting, of
very early morning. And what had made her suppose there weren't many birds up here in the mountains? There must be millions of them shouting
outside now.

Suddenly the day seemed so fresh and new and
beautiful, Jody couldn't stay in bed another minute.
She threw back her blanket and jumped up. The
air coming through her window was sweet and

cold. She poked her head through the curtains to get a better look at this lovely new-hatched world, and there on the path from the creek, scuttling along in a very determined manner, was the MOP!

Chapter Six

She was headed for the house, Jody could see at once. In a minute or two she would be stumping over the porch and banging on the door. And what in the world would happen if Uncle John answered the knock and found himself talking to a live dust mop?

On her bare feet Jody ran silently out of her room and down the stairs. The front door was never locked, and she jerked it open and hoped the rasping squeak it gave wouldn't wake anybody. She opened and shut the screen very carefully because it was apt to bang. Then she flew across the porch and down the steps and along the path. The Mop stopped short and looked shocked.

"I hope you don't customarily run around out-

side in those—those garments," she said sharply.
Jody glanced down at her baby dolls. They had
little blue flowers all over them, and she thought
they were very pretty.

"Oh, it's quite all right this early in the morning,"
she said airily. She didn't know what else to say,
though she wanted to point out that the Mop was
running around outside in nothing at all except her
brown wooden self. "I thought we might go for
a walk, it's so pretty out."

"It's a beautiful morning," said the Mop huffily.
"But it was certainly not the kind of night I had
been led to expect."

"Didn't you hear the fly-by-nights?" asked Jody
innocently.

"Oh, yes, they sang divinely," answered the Mop,
clasping her thin little hands under her nonexistent
chin. Then her voice grew indignant. "It was later,
after they stopped singing, that things grew so
unpleasant. That—that place was hardly more than
a burrow. And the bed was very hard. And it was
right down on the ground, most difficult to get in
and out of. And no facilities, no hot water or soap.
Things running around all night, quite near; one
of them ran right over my feet!" She shuddered
delicately.

"Well," explained Jody, "you were camping out.

I guess that's the way it is when you're camping out."

The Mop drew herself up. "I did not understand that I was 'camping out,' as you say. I understood that I was staying in accommodations provided for visitors who wished to enjoy the outdoors at night. It was uncomfortable and unsuitable for a lone female, and I refuse to stay there any longer. I shall ask your aunt to find more suitable lodgings for me." And she started toward the house.

"No, wait," cried Jody. "Aunt Margaret's still in bed. She wants to be thoroughly rested when the company gets here. Why don't you go back around the bend there, where that little stone bench is, and sit down. There's a beautiful view of the ravine and the rhododendron there. I'll go get Dill; he knows where everything is around here. He'll find a really nice place for you to stay, and we'll take you there ourselves."

The Mop looked unconvinced, but she allowed Jody to lead her to the bench. It was very low, but the Mop still had to struggle to bend in the right places to sit on it. No wonder she had such a hard time in the cave, thought Jody, who knew that Dill's bed was nothing more than a couple of quilts laid on the ground.

Miss Osborne-the-Mop was certainly a curious

sight when she sat. Jody hoped nobody would come along the path and find her perched there. She'd give anybody the screaming meemies.

The sun had risen in the sky now, though the shadows were still long and the air still chilly. What a really beautiful place this is, Jody thought. And she trusted that the Mop was enjoying the towering trees, the blossoming glossy-leaved shrubs, and the awesome big gray rocks, furred with lichen and moss and ferns.

When Jody got back to the house, she could hear Aunt Margaret and Uncle John in the kitchen. She tiptoed up the stairs and into Dill's room. He was asleep on the top bunk bed, and she had to stand on the edge of the bottom bunk and shake him.

It was hard. Waking Dill was never easy. "Lemme 'lone," he growled, putting a pillow over his face.

"Dill, wake up!" whispered Jody fiercely. One of her feet was getting a cramp in it from being curled over the sharp edge of the bed. She grabbed Dill's arm and pinched hard.

"Ouch, ouch, ouch," he muttered. "Go 'way and lemme 'lone."

"Dill!" she cried desperately and twisted her hand in his hair and pulled. She couldn't pull very much because his hair was so short, but it worked.

"For Pete's sake!" he hollered, sitting up and

throwing his pillow across the room. "You're scalping me!"

"Hush, hush," warned Jody. "Oh, Dill, do be quiet. Get up. We have to do something about the Mop. She didn't like the cave, and now she's coming to complain to Aunt Margaret if we don't find her a better place to stay."

"Get me up in the middle of the night and pull all my hair out," grumbled Dill. "Who's the Mop? What's she—oh, the Mop! Jody, good grief, don't let Mother see her! Run quick and stop her!" He jumped to the floor and looked wildly around.

"I have stopped her," said Jody. "She's sitting out on the bench. But she isn't going to be willing to sit there long. She's peeved as a wet hen. We've got to think of something to do with her."

"Take her up the mountain and push her off a cliff," said Dill callously.

"Oh, Dill, I wish you wouldn't talk that way," wailed Jody.

"Well, pushing her off a cliff might be kinder than tying her to a tree and leaving her," answered Dill. "And, Jody, you know we can't just leave her to run around loose."

Jody stared at him. "Oh, what are we going to do?" she asked miserably.

"Don't worry," he told her. "I'll think of something. I'm pretty good at getting out of tight scrapes. You go get dressed. And wear some blue jeans."

Jody dressed hurriedly. She peered into the dim little damp-spotted mirror and slapped at her hair with a brush. The glasses had had to be left at Wolf Town and wouldn't be back for several days. And that's the only good thing that's happened lately, Jody thought. It was nice not to have those heavy old black rims squatting on her nose.

Downstairs Dill was already dressed and eating his cantaloupe. "Mother's putting us up some sandwiches," he informed Jody. "I told her we were going up the mountain and probably would be gone most of the day. She was glad; she's getting ready for her company."

Jody nodded. She ate so fast she could feel large unchewed lumps of cantaloupe under her ribs for an hour afterward. But she knew Aunt Margaret would fuss if they didn't eat—and Jody could practically *hear* the Mop growing more and more impatient out on that bench.

Dill finished first. "I'll get the sandwiches," he said. "You go sit with . . . you know."

Jody gulped the rest of her milk and took half of her piece of toast with her. The Mop was sitting just as Jody had left her. She looked relaxed and contented, and Jody was relieved.

Suddenly it occurred to her that perhaps a night's

sleep had restored her powers. Silently she crept
up behind the Mop. From the back, except for
her little stick arms and legs, it was hard to tell
that the Mop wasn't an ordinary dust mop. So it
ought to be easy, Jody told herself. Nevertheless,
she concentrated with all her muscles. "Be a mop,"
she breathed softly.

For just an instant she thought it had worked.
And then the Mop's head whirled around. "It's very
bad manners to sneak up on people," she snapped.

"Oh, oh," cried Jody, a little startled herself. "I
didn't mean to sneak. It's the path being so thick
with pine needles. And I'm wearing tennis shoes."

She held up her foot for the Mop to see, and just
then Dill came pounding down the path. He was
carrying a very bulky knapsack. What a lot of lunch,
thought Jody.

"Good morning, Miss Mop," he cried gaily. Goodness, thought Jody, I've never known Dill to be so
polite to anybody. He's practically bowing and
scraping and kissing her hand.

"I'm sorry to hear you didn't have a restful night,"
he went on in a horrible mincing voice. "Though
I must say I couldn't tell from looking at you. You
look as fresh as a daisy!"

The Mop was not to be soothed. "You needn't be
so innocent, young man," she scolded. "That was
an unkind trick, to persuade me to stay in that

unpleasant place with all those creatures. I might
have been gnawed on!" And she shivered convul-
sively.

Dill's awful politeness vanished. "Gosh, they're
just deer mice," he exclaimed hotly. "They eat
nuts and seeds and things. They don't gnaw on mo—
on people. And I don't think it's such an unpleasant
place. I've spent lots of nights there. And Uncle
Andrew sleeps there every time he comes to visit.
And even Daddy sleeps there."

The Mop looked at him pensively. "Well, I don't
suppose you meant any harm," she said, sounding
less irritated. "Perhaps you didn't realize that a
spot suitable for vigorous men was not quite the
place for a delicate female. So rough and primitive;
most uncomfortable."

"I'm sorry," said Dill, and he really did sound
contrite. "I guess I'm just used to it."

"And I suppose it is healthful," mused the Mop.
"The fresh mountain air and the brisk temperature."

"Oh, yes," cried Jody. "People are always saying
how healthy the mountain air is. It's very good for
you to sleep in the open, I'm sure it is."

"I wish we'd taken you farther up the mountain,"
Dill put in hastily. "The air up there is just full of
health and minerals and things. And there are lots
of nice places to stay."

"To stay?" asked the Mop. "Not to camp out?"

"Well," said Dill a little uncertainly, "it isn't fancy. But it isn't a cave."

"Oh, I don't object to things being *plain*," explained the Mop. "It's just that I'm not really very strong," she said faintly, putting one hand to her stringy head. "I just really cannot stand up to a very strenuous existence. But I would like to have a pleasant place to stay in the mountains for a few days. It's so beautiful, there's so much of interest to see, the flora and fauna and all. And I'm sure it would be good for my health."

"Well, I was thinking about a sort of mountain cabin," said Dill vaguely.

"Just the thing!" cried the Mop. "Do let's start."

Jody shot Dill an apprehensive glance. Did he truly expect to leave the Mop in that old shack he and Bill Rabun had built last year? She'd have a fit when she saw it, Jody told herself darkly. The cave was better; at least it didn't leak buckets when it rained.

"We can take this path by the creek and then on up the mountain," said Dill, looking relieved. "It's a good day for walking."

"Yes, indeed," murmured the Mop. "A beautiful day. And how lovely the rhododendron is. That pale pink is particularly handsome. I want to get a closer look."

She scurried along the path, and her ridiculous

little legs switched back and forth under her tall skinny body like—like—well, Jody couldn't think like what. But she couldn't watch long without having to turn her head aside and press her hand to her face to keep from laughing.

"Are you really going to take her to the shack?" she whispered to Dill. He nodded grimly. "She'll have a real duck fit," prophesied Jody.

"Well, she'll just have to have it," said Dill. "Nobody can hear her taking on up there. And can you think of anything else to do with her? I thought we could fix up the roof with some branches and bark. It isn't going to rain anytime soon, anyway. I brought a blanket in the knapsack, and there's an old cot still in there. We'll fix the place up for her as good as we can today, and tomorrow we can bring up a camp stool and a few things. If it's cleaned up, it shouldn't be too bad." He sighed. "We can keep her up here this summer, but come fall I don't know what we'll do."

For a while they walked in melancholy silence, faced with the prospect of spending the rest of their lives caring for the Mop and hiding her from the eyes of the world.

Oh, dear, oh, dear, wailed Jody to herself. It's all Dill's fault. I shouldn't have listened to him.

"It's all your fault," said Dill bitterly. "You never should have listened to me."

"There's a robin," cried the Mop, pointing at a big rusty-breasted bird scratching in the path ahead of them. "Do come along, you two, you miss everything poking along like that."

"It was *not* my fault," Jody began, but Dill wasn't listening. "If she isn't strong, I'm a chimpanzee's cousin," he said crossly and hurried to catch up with the Mop as she hopped up the winding trail.

Jody still lagged behind. Maybe she would be way down the mountain when the Mop got her first look at her "cabin" and had her fit. Well, it was a lovely day, and that was the only consolation Jody could think of. The sun was bright and the air was cool, and though they had left the creek behind, they could still occasionally hear it talking and murmuring off in the distance. They climbed steadily and as they went higher the path became rougher and less well marked.

Once in a while they got a glimpse of the surrounding peaks, blue and lavender and shadowed as they rose against the sky. The tops of the tallest mountains were swathed in mist as though they were wearing white silk turbans.

The Mop had left the path to observe an azalea bush. Dill stood waiting for her, and now Jody caught up with him. She had just opened her mouth to resume the argument about whose fault it was, when he suddenly seized her arm.

"Listen," he hissed. "Somebody's coming!"

There was a noise almost beside them in the underbrush, somebody shouted out roughly, and then there was the deafening roar of a shot!

Chapter Seven

"Hey, watch out!" shouted Dill. The Mop squealed and began to jump up and down. Jody was so fascinated by this peculiar sight that she did nothing at all. Whoever was in the bushes yelled, "Low-down good-for-nothin' varmints! Now git!" And the gun sounded again.

"Mr. Poteet! Mr. Poteet!" shrieked Dill. "Quit shooting! It's me, Dill Tracy!"

There was a great rustling in the bushes and then an old man, ragged and dirty, carrying a shotgun and accompanied by a skinny and melancholy hound dog, stepped out of the laurel and arrowwood. From under a battered old wide-brimmed hat he peered this way and that and finally pointed a finger toward Jody.

"That you, young'un?" he asked. "Boy, is that you?"

"Here I am, Mr. Poteet," Dill answered, moving forward. "That's my cousin, Jody Ransom, over there. And we've got a lady with us, Miss—Miss Mop."

The old man leaned in the Mop's direction, swinging his head and shoulders up and down like a big ragged bear. "Whar?" he asked, staring nearsightedly around. "Whar's she at?"

"Right there beside Jody," Dill said. "She's visiting. She isn't very well. We thought the air up here might be good for her."

The old man walked right up to Jody and then swept his hat from his head. "Howdo, ma'am," he said politely. "I'm proud to make your acquaintance. It ain't often I get to see a lady in these parts."

The Mop drew herself up into her usual posture of offended dignity. "Well, that's small wonder if you're going to shoot at people continually," she said tartly.

"Well, if I'd knowed it was you, I wouldn't have shot," the old man answered in a hurt tone. "I warn't after you, I was after them no-good Hadley boys. They knowed I was settin' out for Wolf Town, and they aim to come wreck my place whilst I'm gone."

He glared all around, with a specially fierce glare
for a couple of suspicious-looking bushes.

"I don't think you heard the Hadley boys," Dill
soothed him. "It was just us. We haven't seen or
heard another person on the trail."

"That right?" asked Mr. Poteet. "Well, don't
pay no 'tention to old Betsy here, anyways. Her
bark's worse'n her bite. Fact is, they ain't no lead
in her, just powder. Down to the hardware store,
they won't sell me no shot; claim I can't see too
good. Dern foolishness. I can see a fly's eye at fifty
paces."

But Jody could tell it wasn't so. The old man obviously had some sort of eye trouble and could barely make out his hand before his face. No wonder Dill wasn't afraid to introduce the Mop to him.

"But I wouldn't never shoot at a lady," the old man assured the Mop. "Partic'lar not one as warn't feelin' too pert." He stared at her earnestly. "You do look puny. You ain't got much flesh on you, for a fact, and you ain't a good color. Likely you got a bad heart."

The Mop began to languish at once. She leaned on Jody and said faintly, "I am simply not at all strong. I wouldn't be surprised to find I have a weak heart. I came to the mountains in the hope that the pure and invigorating air would help me."

"Why, hit's the truth," cried Mr. Poteet. "A little rest up here in the hills will do you a world of good. This here air is the healthiest air in creation. I just breathe in a big gulp night and mornin' and it's such good, pure air I don't hardly have to worry about doin' any breathin' in between. It's all the medicine a body needs, 'cept maybe a little yarb tonic onct in a while. I make a fine yarb tonic myself. Left a big new-made jar of it up to my house just this mornin'. If'n I was to home, I'd give you a dose or two. It's a famous remedy."

Dill made a face. He'd had a taste of Mr. Poteet's herb tonic.

Mr. Poteet was reluctant to let a patient slide through his fingers. "I'm headin' down to Wolf Town to see my brother and sister," he told the Mop. "I won't be gone but a day or so. You come by and see me first of next week and I'll give you some tonic."

"How kind of you," answered the Mop. "It is nice to feel that someone appreciates my delicate state of health. After all, these children . . . sometimes I don't believe . . ." her voice trailed off weakly.

"Oh, now, ma'am, you got nothin' to worry about," cried Mr. Poteet. "I promise you, a few days up here and a couple of spoonfuls of my tonic and you'll be right as rain, I take my oath on it. Where'll you be stayin'?"

The Mop looked questioningly at Dill. Dill looked up at the sky and craned his neck. "Isn't that a hawk going over," he asked in a terribly interested voice.

Mr. Poteet rolled a crafty eye first at Dill and then at the Mop. "Tell you what," he said slowly, "how come you don't stay at my place? I ain't fixin' to be there. It's a real nice place, and you could have it all to yourself. And you could have the tonic. It's settin' on the back of the stove, a big jar full. If'n you was there to look after my hens and make sure the Hadley boys don't bust things up, why then I

could visit a mite longer with my brother down in
Wolf Town."

"How much?" asked Dill, who was well ac-
quainted with Mr. Poteet.

"Quarter," answered the old man promptly. "And
quarter for the tonic."

"It's a deal," said Dill, looking relieved. "How
long will you be gone?"

"Oh, two, three days," Mr. Poteet said vaguely.
"Or not so long. A month most likely. I'll be gettin'
on now."

"Won't you need to go back to your house and
pack?" asked Jody. She wondered what kind of
house he had.

"Pack what?" asked Mr. Poteet, squinting at her.

"Well, you know, your clothes and all," Jody explained.

Mr. Poteet looked puzzled. "I'm a-wearin' my
clothes," he said finally. And then he started on
down the path, trailed by the hound and using the
shotgun as a sort of cane to feel for obstacles.

"Will he be all right?" asked Jody worriedly.

"Sure," Dill answered. "He walks this trail a
couple of times a week."

Now the Mop spoke up. "A mountain cabin certainly sounds peaceful and quaint and restful," she
said. "But will it be safe? Suppose the Hadley boys
do come around?"

"We'll stay with you in the daytime," Jody comforted her. "I'm sure you'll be all right."

But secretly she was a little anxious herself. The Hadley boys sounded dangerous. She didn't know what they would do if anybody tried to "tear up the place."

"You don't have to worry. The Hadley boys moved away from the mountain about ten years ago," Dill told them. "Mr. Poteet just uses them as an excuse when he wants to start shooting and stirring up a little excitement. Nobody but him lives up here, and once in a while he gets lonesome. He sort of makes up a feud with the Hadley boys to keep himself company."

"Oh, well, then," said the Mop. "I shall be quite pleased to help Mr. Poteet out by staying at his place and feeding his hens. A fine old gentleman and a most understanding person. How sad that he appears to be losing his sight. Is it far to his house?"

"Not much farther," replied Dill. "About half an hour's walk. The path just keeps on going to his house and then it mostly stops. Hardly anybody comes up here and he's almost at the top of the mountain."

"The top of the mountain! How wonderful that sounds!" cried the Mop, and she trotted on ahead looking eagerly from side to side of the trail.

"Is Mr. Poteet's cabin nice?" asked Jody in a low voice.

"Well, it's better than the shack," Dill answered. "It doesn't leak, anyway. At least not very much. And it's got a floor. It isn't too awful. But she'll have to stay there. We promised Mr. Poteet. The hens, remember?"

That had been a smart move, Jody had to admit.

"Now just look!" cried the Mop, bending perilously down and peering at a little clump of flowers by the edge of the path. Dill and Jody looked. The flowers were small and white and waxy, and the leaves were dark green, spotted and streaked with white. Jody had often seen these curious blooms before, but she hadn't thought to ask anybody what they were.

"That's double-your-money-back," explained the Mop now. "That's the common name, of course. I can't recall the scientific name at the moment. An unusual profusion of blooms. For this section of the country, of course," she added.

Dill nudged Jody, and Jody said, "Ouch." If they didn't hurry up and get rid of the Mop, Jody's ribs were going to be completely mangled.

"I wonder how it is," she murmured as once more the Mop scurried ahead of them, "that the Mop knows the names of some things, like robins and rhododendron, but other things she has these made-up names for. Fruit-frosted cupcake!" she said scorn-fully.

"What it is, see," explained Dill, "she's supposed to know lots, like your old Miss Osborne does. But really she just knows what you know, Jody, and you're awful ignorant. So when she comes to some-thing you don't know, she has to make it up out of things that sort of seeped into her when she was in the pantry or the grocery store or someplace. See?"

"I am *not* ignorant," said Jody hotly. But she sup-posed Dill must be right, especially after what hap-pened at the spring where they stopped to drink the cold water. At least Dill and Jody drank. The Mop amused herself by poking at an old half-rotted, fungus-covered log.

Suddenly she gave a little yelp. The children turned to look. A big piece of bark had slipped from the log, and there in the middle of the decayed wood, among the bewildered beetles and sowbugs, sat a small glistening black-and-gold spotted crea-ture with a long tail and four stubby legs. Its head was lifted high, and they could see its tiny smooth-skinned throat pulse in and out with surprise and fear.

"Is it a lizard?" asked Jody.

"Naw," said Dill, who spent so much time clam-

bering over rocks and logs that he was well ac-
quainted with lizards. "It's real different from a
lizard. It's some kind of something else."

"Of course, it's something else," said the Mop in
her brisk teacher's voice. "It's an inner seal. A gold
inner seal."

"Oh," said Dill, looking a little confused. "I wonder what it eats under there? Dead wood?"

The salamander lifted a cautious foot and began
to crawl slowly around the log. "It eats ingredients,"
the Mop told him. "Active and inert ingredients.
And beetles."

Dill fitted the bark carefully back over the log to
shelter the little creature. He didn't dare look at
Jody. He knew if he did, they'd both burst out
laughing.

The path wound on up the mountainside. The
trees were more scattered, but the laurel and rhododendron were taller and thicker than ever.

"Look yonder, you can see Mr. Poteet's house,"
said Dill, pointing. Jody and the Mop glanced up
at the little peaked gray-shingled roof poking up out
of the dark green shrubbery. It really did look
quaint and peaceful and pretty. Jody began to feel
better. As long as the Mop had to be more or less
imprisoned up here on the mountain top, Jody
wanted her to have a pleasant place to stay.

But, when they came closer, they saw that around

Mr. Poteet's house the laurel and rhododendron had been cleared away for a good space. This was unfortunate, Jody thought. It gave you time to get the full effect before you even got there.

They all stopped short, staring.

"Oh, my goodness," said the Mop in disbelieving tones. "Oh, my goodness gracious!"

Chapter Eight

"Oh, Dill," exclaimed Jody reproachfully.

"It's got worse since I was here last, lots worse," said Dill hastily. "Honest it has."

Well, it couldn't have been very good, even then, Jody told herself. Because it must have taken a long time for one cabin and clearing to get this ramshackle and disreputable-looking. The house leaned to one side as though a good wind would blow it over. And the little porch leaned the other way as though it had quarreled with the cabin. At the dirty windows cobwebs made a thick screen, and from the half-open door a long trail of empty bottles, elderly shoes, rags, and newspapers slid down the sagging boards of the porch and spilled out onto the sandy earth, where three or four bedraggled hens squeezed their wretched way through rusty fenders, cans, broken pots, scraggly weeds, old tires, odds and ends of lumber, and a good many other things that were not immediately identifiable.

The Mop just stood there, looking stunned. Jody wondered if she might faint.

Dill gave a long, low whistle. "Gosh," he said finally. Then he turned to the Mop. "I'm sorry," he said. "I just didn't know it was this bad. Cross my heart, I didn't. But you got to stay. We promised Mr. Poteet, remember?"

"Of course, I shall stay," answered the Mop. "I never had anything else in mind. I certainly wouldn't go back on my word to Mr. Poteet." She turned her head slowly, looking around. "It's just that I didn't have the faintest idea it would be like this. I had thought . . . quaint cabin . . . peace and quiet . . ." Her voice faded sadly; her thin shoulders drooped. All at once Jody felt terribly sorry for her.

"Well, it *is* a lovely place," she cried, taking the Mop's bony little hand in hers. "Look at the view. And those nice white flowers over there. And—and we could clean it up. It would be a sweet little cabin if it was tidied up, I think. Dill and I could do it, couldn't we, Dill?"

The Mop took a step forward. She suddenly held up her head, and a gleam came into her eye. "We

certainly could clean it up," she exclaimed. Jody
had an odd sensation. Cleaning up is what mops are
for, she thought, and didn't know whether her sug-
gestion had been a good one or not.

"It would be a good deed," the Mop went on en-
thusiastically. "Of course, poor Mr. Poteet doesn't
realize how run-down his property has become. I
suppose he's too shortsighted to see it, and perhaps
too old and feeble to do much about it even if he
could see. Yes, I really think rehabilitating this place
would be a fine, neighborly thing to do."

Dill looked doubtful, but he said nothing.

The Mop picked her way through the debris to
the little porch, and the children followed to peer
through the door into the dimness of the cabin.
Jody caught her breath. It was even worse inside and
really amazingly dirty.

There was only one room, plus a little lean-to. A
big fireplace took up most of one side of the room,
and a little monkey stove for cooking stood beside it.
Against the opposite wall stood a vast bed, covered
with a homemade shuck mattress and a grimy blanket. And that was all the furniture there was. A
couple of small barrels stood around as if Mr. Poteet
had used them for tables or chairs, and a rocking
chair with one rocker broken off leaned discon-
solately in a corner.

But everywhere were bottles, baskets, boxes, pails,

wheels, cans, ropes, rags, pots and pans, stacks of paper, picture frames, parts of sewing machines, washtubs, scrub boards, jars, and millions of other things, all broken and useless and all covered with cobwebs, soot, grease, and what looked like generous splashes of Mr. Poteet's herb tonic.

"The first thing we have to do is take that bed outside," said the Mop.

"The first thing we have to do is eat lunch," said Dill firmly. "I'm starving."

Jody was hungry too. But as they sat on the porch and ate, somehow the sandwiches and cookies and lemonade didn't taste as good as she had thought they would. We should have eaten down by the spring, she told herself. Who could have any appetite in this ugly place? And with her toe she pushed a rusty can and two muddy chicken feathers out of sight under the porch.

Dill, however, didn't seem to mind. He kept right on eating while he poked around, finding all kinds of things that made him exclaim with delight: a coil of wire and an old automobile battery, a bag full of nuts and screws, and a bedpost with carved vines curling up it.

When the lunch was all eaten, the children went back into the cabin.

Poor Mr. Poteet, thought Jody suddenly. What a horrid way to live!

On a nail by the door hung a worn and patched gray overcoat. Was this really all the old man's clothes except those he was wearing? By the stove, with the chicken feed, sat a tin pail full of corn meal, a bag of squashy potatoes, and a bucket of lard. Was this what he ate, day in and day out?

She gave a little shiver. "What's the matter?" asked Dill, coming up beside her.

"I was just thinking about Mr. Poteet," she explained. "I feel so sorry for him, living in this awful place, with nothing good to eat and no clothes and everything so ugly."

"Gosh, I don't think it's so awful," said Dill, looking around. "I think it's kind of nice. And I expect he likes it. He's got all these interesting things around, right where he wants them. He doesn't ever have to think about putting things away in boxes or closets. When he wants something, why, there it is, right where he left it. Neat-o!"

He pulled an ancient leather briefcase out from under some wire screening. "And when he gets ready to go someplace, he just goes. He doesn't have to worry about locking up or putting things away or packing. Good grief, when we come up here you ought to see the packing we do; for days my mother is packing and packing and packing. We just about go crazy with all that packing. And when we go back to town it's even worse."

He wiped some cobwebs off his hands. "Of course," he added, "I don't guess I'd want things to be this dirty. And I wouldn't like just eating those crumby potatoes and corn bread the way Mr. Poteet does. But I think he likes them."

Jody thought this over. Maybe Dill was right. But she certainly wouldn't like it, living this way. Not even if she could have fried chicken and lemon pie every day.

"The way to do this is to sort the stuff out," Dill explained, picking up an old door mat and discovering a ladder with only two rungs beneath it. "You know, stack up the papers to be burned and the cans to throw away and all this good junk—"

"We have to move the bed outside first," the Mop interrupted. "I will not spend a night in this house while it is in this condition. I will sleep under the stars. I do wish that mattress weren't so dirty."

"We've got a blanket to cover it with," said Jody. She wondered if they could get that bed out of the house at all. The square dark wooden posts were massive, and they looked as if they weighed tons.

And she and Dill did have a struggle getting the headboard and footboard outside, but fortunately there were no slats or springs, just a sort of rope sling crisscrossed between the sides of the bed to lay the mattress on.

They set up the bed under a big sugar maple tree.

"I hope it doesn't rain," Jody whispered to Dill.

"Well, she was the one who wanted to have it outside," he answered. "Besides I don't think it's going to rain for a while. Actually I don't see why she'd mind getting wet."

Jody giggled. "She's a dust mop, not a wet mop," she said, and Dill grinned.

While she spread the blanket over the grubby mattress, Jody watched Dill and the Mop. They both seemed quite happy to be rooting around among the boxes and jars, but she had an idea they had very different reasons for doing it.

As for Jody, she was feeling terribly discouraged. They could never get this place cleaned up. Whatever had made her suggest it? And how did the summer manage to get worse and worse? Scrubbing and mopping and brushing! What a ghastly way to spend your vacation!

The Mop trotted through the door of the cabin and then turned to call them in after her.

"I think Dill is quite right," she said thoughtfully. "We must organize a plan. The thing to do is get all the papers and rags and things of that order and burn them. This afternoon, quickly, while the ground is still damp from the recent rains. And then we can begin to dispose of the other things."

There was a surprising quantity of burnable things. A stack of twenty-year-old magazines, wads of newspapers, some rolls of wallpaper, mildewed and stained. And rags—sleeves without shirts, and shirts without sleeves, single socks and gloves, and thousands of greasy, dingy objects of unidentifiable origin. They formed a huge pile, and the fire made such a smoke that Dill was worried.

"If the forest ranger comes along to investigate this, we'll really be in a pickle," he muttered to Jody.

But the forest ranger didn't come. And though the Mop kept finding more pieces of paper, hidden under bushes or wedged between the boards of the house, eventually the fire burned down to ashes, to iridescent flakes of paper and wads of smoldering cloth.

They dug up some of the damp, sandy soil in the clearing and spread it over the remains of the fire, and Dill stamped it down firmly.

"We have to go now," Jody told the Mop a little timidly. "We have to be back home in time for supper. I do hope you won't be lonely tonight."

"Nonsense," said the Mop. "I shall go right to bed and be well rested for tomorrow's work."

"Me, too," said Dill. "I'm tired out." And he yawned.

"We'll be up here as early in the morning as we can get here," Jody said. And when they started down the path toward home, she turned to look back

at the grotesque little figure perched on the edge
of Mr. Poteet's enormous bed.

"Does she sleep?" wondered Jody aloud. "Or does
she just lie there? And what does she think about
while she's lying there?"

"She thinks about mopping," said Dill briefly.

But Jody didn't agree with him. A person who
was a mixture of dust mop and Jody Ransom and
the supermarket at Wolf Town and Miss Osborne
and the Sorcerer's Apprentice surely must have some
very unusual things to think about as she lay "under
the stars."

Well, I guess we'll never know, Jody thought,
and pelted on down the path.

The next morning the Mop's "organized plan"
went into effect. Mostly it seemed to mean disposing
of all the useless, broken, dirty things that cluttered
the cabin.

Dill and the Mop argued over the question of
what was "no-good" and what wasn't.

"Look here," Dill would cry, holding up some
filthy object. "A perfectly good plastic seat cover."
Or hot-water bottle or electric razor case or whatever it was.

"Throw it away," the Mop would say sharply.

And Dill would protest, "It's only got a couple

of teeny holes in it; we could mend it with Scotch tape."

And then the Mop would stamp her tiny foot and glare from under her stringy hair, and eventually Dill would shrug and say, "Oh, well." And the precious item would join the other things to be disposed of.

And this brought up further argument. Dill was all for dumping these things from the house out in the yard. And Jody too thought this was the most sensible plan. The yard was close at hand and nothing could make it look much worse. Jody supposed that secretly Dill hoped something would happen before they had to clean up the yard. She did herself. She couldn't think what it would be, but she hoped it was something.

Now the Mop shook her dusty head. "There's no point in increasing the disorder," she pointed out. She had that gleam in her eye that made Dill say they would end up scrubbing the whole mountain, dusting the huckleberries, and putting wax on the acorns.

"Well, what will we do with the rubbish?" asked Jody.

"Bury it," answered the Mop. "Dill can dig some deep holes, and we'll bury it all."

"Are you out of your mind?" cried Dill indignantly. "I can't dig any deep holes around here; it's too rocky. And besides, I'd be digging holes from now till Christmas to bury all this stuff."

"Don't shout," whispered the Mop. "It makes me feel quite faint." She shut her eyes and pressed her hand to her skinny chest. "Then I shall do it myself, though I shall probably make myself ill."

And she went and fetched an old spade out of the lean-to and began to dig, stopping every now and then to sigh and hold her head. The ground was certainly rocky and very hard.

"She's not ever going to get a hole big enough to bury her toe in at that rate," Dill told Jody.

"Oh, Dill, you have to think of something to do with this stuff," Jody cried. "We can't sit here and watch her doing that."

"Oh, all right," said Dill. "I guess I have to."

So of course he did. He thought of the sinkhole. It was right back of Mr. Poteet's house, a rocky chasm which fell away into a black bottomless depth where some flaw in the mountain's rocky structure had opened a shaft far down into the earth.

To get there you had to go around behind the cabin and through the weedy clearing and then about fifty feet along a little path that twisted between laurel bushes until you came to the gaping hole. Jody and Dill traveled this path so many times during the next few days, Jody complained that even after she was asleep at night her feet kept right on walking over it.

Armload after armload of rubbish went racketing hollowly down into the earth. Dill saw a lot of it go with a pang. "I should have buried it," he told Jody. "Then I might have been able to dig some of it up later."

Jody grinned and went back for another load. She didn't want any of these things, and actually she was enjoying herself immensely. It was fun to take up a big basketful of broken bottles and rusty cans and odd wheels and send it echoing down into the dark. You could hear things breaking and splintering as they bounced from side to side of the shaft. The sounds grew fainter and fainter and then stopped about the time the load hit Australia, Jody thought.

Dill ran and caught up with her. "We should have thrown the Mop down there," he said, but Jody knew he was only teasing.

As a matter of fact, both the children were having a good time. As a taskmaster the Mop had only one serious flaw. She didn't get tired. And she didn't understand what Jody and Dill meant when they said they wanted to rest.

She herself worked very hard, trotting back and forth with boxes full of refuse. She was very strong and could carry a heavier load than Dill even, though her legs were so short she couldn't—like Jody and Dill—step over weeds, bushes, and piles of debris. Instead, she had to skirt around them with her tiny steps, so that the walk back and forth to the sinkhole took her much longer.

However, her skinny little leathery wooden arms and legs never seemed to get weary. When the children insisted on stopping for a rest, she would hold her head and say faintly, "Yes, I mustn't overdo."

But no sooner had they settled down in some

shady spot than she would jump up, saying eagerly, "Now we've rested. Back to work."

The only thing that saved them from dying of exhaustion, Dill said, was that the Mop was so easily distracted. She had sharp eyes and ears and she saw many things that the children missed.

"Look," she would call as she rounded a huckleberry bush. "A butterfly just emerging from its chrysalis!" And Jody and Dill would welcome the opportunity to sit down and watch that limp be-

draggled ugly object squeezing out of its little
wizened case. It crouched in the sun and stretched
until its wings flowered into brightly scaled expanses
of amber and silver and copper.

"Oh, how pretty," Jody cried.

"What kind is it?" asked Dill.

The Mop cocked her head. "That's a washday
product, if I'm not mistaken," she answered, and
Dill poked Jody again.

Jody and Dill soon learned to do some sharp looking of their own, since this was to be the only way
they ever got a chance to catch a breath. The pleated
silky underside of a toadstool, a spider swathing its
prey in a band of white silk, a snail leaving a glassy
trail across some moss, ants moving their white eggs
from one hiding place to another—all these things
were fun to see besides slowing down the Mop's
whirlwind activities for a while.

Little by little the house was cleared of everything
in it. Only the stove squatted forlornly by the gaping black fireplace when the Mop and the two grimy
children returned from the last trip to the sinkhole.

"Jeepers," groaned Dill, "I'm glad that's done."

"Yes," agreed the Mop eagerly, "because now the
hard work begins."

Dill rolled his eyes at Jody. "What does she call
hard work?" he muttered. "Are we going to have to
vacuum-clean the whole mountain?"

Chapter Nine

Jody pried the wooden top off the well and laid it
on the ground. As she lowered the bucket toward
the water, she sniffed deeply. There was honeysuckle blooming somewhere near. Through the
spicy scent of a mountain morning its sweet fra-
grance drifted past her every now and then as she
worked. Even the mossy smell from the well was
pleasant, Jody thought as she leaned over to watch
the bucket come up through the little fringe of
ferns. The Mop would have enjoyed all these aro-
matic things if she'd been able to.

Jody emptied the bucket into a big round black
pot and then once again lowered it squeakily into
the cool dimness of the well. She didn't hurry. There
was already one pot of water heating on the stove.

It was certainly different from cleaning up at home, where you just turned on the hot water and it gushed from the faucet. Here you had to gather the firewood and start the fire, draw five buckets of water to fill the pot, and then wait for the pot to boil.

Maybe that's why Mr. Poteet doesn't bother with cleaning, she thought. But I like doing it. And I like cleaning the cabin. She grinned a little, remembering the "sweeping day." She didn't suppose it was the kind of thing Mr. Poteet would ever do. Even the Mop had found it a little strenuous and "most undignified." But Jody and Dill had had a wonderful time, whirling around the cabin with brooms, sweeping down the walls and ceiling, shrieking like witches, giggling and bringing down showers of dirt and raising hurricane clouds of dust.

Aunt Margaret had been something less than pleased with them when they got home. "Where in the world have you been to get so filthy?" she cried. "And what in the world are you up to, going up the mountain every day?" she added suspiciously. "And with *brooms*. Are you talking flying lessons from someone up there?"

"Well," explained Dill hastily, "we found this old cabin and we thought we'd like to use it, sort of like a clubhouse, you know? But it was sure enough dirty, so we swept it out some. That's all."

"Oh," said Aunt Margaret. "I hope it's safe. The roof won't fall in on you or anything, will it?"

"No'm," answered Dill. "It's got a pretty good roof."

And nothing more was said. But Dill had to sneak into town with Mr. Rabun one day to buy the soaps and scrub brushes and cleaners the Mop said they must have.

"I don't want Mother seeing all this," he explained to Jody. "If she finds out I'm washing anything, she'll think I'm sick or losing my mind or something."

"Did you see Mr. Poteet in Wolf Town?" asked Jody.

"No," answered Dill. "And I was glad I didn't. I didn't want him to see me buying soap, either."

"Why not?" asked Jody, but Dill didn't answer. Instead, he showed her a quarter he had in his pocket.

"That's all I've got left out of three-weeks' allowance," he said gloomily. "I can't see why people are so worried about being clean all the time when it costs so much. Being dirty is easier and a whole lot cheaper."

Jody frowned. She would have to give Dill part of the money she had saved for Daddy's birthday present.

"I wish I could still work miracles," she com-

plained. "Then I could just turn some of Mr. Poteet's old jars and cans into scrub brushes and detergents."

"If you could still work miracles," retorted Dill acidly, "you could just turn the Mop back into a mop, and that would be the end of it. We wouldn't have to fix up Mr. Poteet's place." He wondered a minute. "But it isn't as bad as I thought it would be. I mean it's not like real work. Not like making a bed or straightening out a drawer. It's something you can really light into and do with all your might and main. And when you get through, you can see what you've done. It really makes a difference."

Well, thought Jody, as she emptied the last bucket into the pot, actually it's more like play than work. Now they were scrubbing the walls. With hot water and cleanser and brushes, they scoured the rough wooden boards in great sudsy circles and wide bubbly streaks. To rinse it they just threw buckets of cold well water against the walls, splattering and showering each other in the process. The Mop followed behind them sedately sweeping the pools and puddles and rivulets of water out the door.

It might not be the way most people would do it, but it certainly was effective. The cabin was beginning to look like a place to be lived in. Jody was proud of what they had done.

However, right now she needed some help with

this pot of water. It was too heavy for her to lift by herself.

"Dill!" she yelled. "Come help with the water!"

Dill came unhurriedly out of the cabin. He was barefooted and his legs were streaked with dust and dirty water. Jody giggled.

"You're such a funny color you look like you'd been taking Mr. Poteet's tonic," she said. For the Mop had discovered Mr. Poteet's bottle of fresh herb tonic almost as soon as they entered the cabin. And she had faithfully taken a large dose every day.

The children had been puzzled at first. How was the Mop, who did not eat and apparently could not swallow, going to take this big tablespoonful of muddy brown liquid? But as Dill said, you could count on the Mop. She poured part of the tonic into the palm of her narrow little hand and then solemnly rubbed it all over herself, up and down her thin little arms and legs and her polelike body.

It turned her a curious earthy color and gave her a very pungent odor. Perhaps it was just as well she didn't have a sense of smell, Jody thought.

Now Dill looked down at his dust-smeared legs and laughed. "I look a lot worse than that," he admitted. "Haul up another bucket and let's have a drink."

There was a dipper, so old and rusty Jody wouldn't use it. Instead, she used one of Aunt Mar-

garet's pink plastic cups out of the lunch basket they
brought with them every day.

The water was delicious. In fact, it tasted so good
that Dill said it was a shame to waste it on house-
cleaning.

"Listen," he said now, pausing with the dripping
dipper in his hand.

A bird was calling. That isn't singing, Jody
thought. Not that series of loud hollow clucks as
though someone was striking two wooden blocks
together. And yet there was something beautiful
about it, something wild and strange and exciting
that made her long to hear it again, when the clucks
had speeded up and then slowed down and stopped.

"I know what that is," said Dill. "That's a yellow-
billed cuckoo."

"No," said Jody, "I think it's a patent pending."

Dill shook his head. "I'm not playing the game,"
he said. The game was something they played when
the Mop wasn't around to hear. They gave Moplike
names to the birds and animals and plants they saw
around the cabin. A hummingbird was a minimum
daily requirement, sourwood trees were punch here
trees, and once when they had seen a doe and fawn
scampering up the trail, Dill had told Jody they
were a gross weight and a net weight. Jody had been
too thrilled to say anything. Real live deer! She'd
never expected to see any except in zoos.

Now Dill said, "It really is a yellow-billed cuckoo. Uncle Andrew told me so."

Jody was astonished. "I thought a cuckoo was a made-up bird to go in a clock," she said.

Dill was scornful. "Of course not, silly," he said. "There are lots of cuckoos, and this is one of Uncle Andrew's favorite birds. I've seen him. He's long and skinny and has white spots in his tail."

And just then the bird flew from its perch and swooped in front of the children. It was certainly long and slim, and the white spots flashed.

"I still think it's a patent pending," said Jody. "And the white spots are registered trade marks."

"Maybe so," said Dill with a grin. "But I tell you one thing. We better hurry and get this finished and move the bed back into the house. Mr. Poteet calls that bird a rain crow, and he says when it hollers close to the house, it means rain. And from the way things look around here, he's right."

And he was right. It took forty-eight hours for him to be right, and then he was right with a vengeance. The chilly rain poured down.

Fortunately the roof only leaked in one place.

By that time the cabin and its furnishings had all been scrubbed clean. The windows gleamed—though a few panes were missing—and the floors, if they did not shine, were at least scoured almost white. The big bed had been waxed and polished and set up in the corner, with the mattress cover washed and boiled and filled with fresh shucks provided by Mr. Rabun. A little cracked pitcher full of flowers stood on the mantel, a bright blanket was spread over the bed, and a picture of a magnificent blue lake surrounded by snow-capped purple mountains, rescued from the debris only a little stained and torn, was pinned to one wall.

The Mop looked contentedly around. "Now this is the way a mountain cabin ought to look," she said approvingly. She was perched on a barrel, making curtains out of some flour sacks they had found. She had proved to be very talented with a needle—she didn't get that from me, thought Jody, who couldn't sew on a button in spite of much effort and many tears—and had even sewed together a very dilapidated rag rug which now lay on the floor, looking somewhat dingy and dubious but reasonably whole.

Jody and Dill were mending the broken rocking chair. At least, Jody was holding it and Dill was banging away with the hammer.

"Hold it tight," grumbled Dill. "It's going to be crooked if you keep letting go of it that way."

"I can't hold it tight," snapped Jody. "You keep looking like you're going to hit me with the hammer, and I'm scared."

"Don't quarrel, children," said the Mop. "Doesn't the rain on the roof sound wonderful?"

Jody cocked an ear. The heavy drops drummed and thrummed on the shingles, now growing louder and then almost dying away. It did sound wonderful. It was funny how the Mop always noticed such things.

"I hope it doesn't last too long, however," said the Mop, holding her needle in her skinny fingers. "Now that we've finished the house, I'm eager to start on the garden."

"On the garden!" cried Jody.

"You mean this crumby clearing?" asked Dill. "Mr. Poteet's yard? I don't think you better. I don't think he's going to like this."

"Nonsense," said the Mop in her briskest voice. "Of course, such a very pleasant old gentleman doesn't enjoy living in squalor. If he were capable of cleaning the place up, he would have, long ago."

"Gosh," muttered Dill to Jody, "I think she's got Mr. Poteet all wrong."

But he and Jody knew there wasn't much they could do to stop the Mop once she made up her mind. They had to keep her up here where no one could see her, and since cleaning up seemed to be what made her happy, then cleaning up was what they had to let her do.

When they arrived at the cabin the next morn-

ing, Jody had to admit the Mop had a point. The
rain had ceased, but the day was still dark, and the
little gray cabin looked so dismal and pathetic and
bedraggled, Jody didn't believe anybody could want
it that way.

The Mop was already working, carrying armloads
of rusty cans and old shoes to the sinkhole. As they
walked into the yard, she went by with an ancient
tire, rolling it like a hoop beside her as she scurried
along on her short stick legs. Her stringy hair
flopped around her head, her tiny knees pumped
up and down, her arms flailed the air as she went.
Dill grinned as he watched. Then as she went faster
and faster he turned his head to hide his laughter.
And when she disappeared among the laurel bushes,
he collapsed on the porch and roared aloud.

"Oh, Dill, that's cruel," said Jody, who was having a struggle not to burst out laughing herself. "She
can't help being funny-looking."

"She—she—she can't hear me; she's too far away,"
gasped Dill, holding his stomach. He sat up and
wiped his eyes and let the last few hiccuping giggles
out of his chest. "I know she can't help it," he said
finally, "but I can't help laughing at her, either.
Those awful little legs, and that hair—I can't stand
it," and he rolled over on his back and dissolved
into helpless chuckles once again.

This episode seemed to put him in a good humor,

however, and he got up and joined Jody and the Mop in the parade back and forth between the clearing and the sinkhole.

There was really an amazing amount of debris in the yard. Jody and Dill were both glad now that the Mop had made them dispose of what was inside the cabin and not add it to the accumulation already in the clearing.

"It must have taken Mr. Poteet a long time to acquire all this," said Jody one morning as she swept up three old bottles, a long wire spring such as is used on screen doors, part of a roller skate, a saucepan with no bottom, the tattered remains of a dictionary, and some burned-out spark plugs. "I wonder how in the world he got it all and what in the world he meant to do with it?"

"He collected it," said Dill. "And he didn't mean to do anything with it. He just liked to have it around. It made him feel good to know it was there."

He said this in an ominous tone that worried Jody Was it right to clean up Mr. Poteet's place? Not that they really had any choice. The Mop was getting to be a real nagger. And if they didn't do exactly what she wanted them to, she got mad and announced she was going to faint or have a heart attack, and the children almost had to do it.

She herself worked the hardest of all. As a matter of fact, she worked all the time. She had given up the pretense of going to bed, and now long after the children had gone she trotted back and forth, working away. And when it got dark, unless there were owls or bats or something to watch she spent the night polishing and scrubbing in the shadows, even things that had already been scrubbed and polished.

"Maybe she'll just work herself right out of existence," said Dill thoughtfully as they shoveled up the last of the refuse.

"I guess not," said Jody. "Because of the healthy mountain air and the herb tonic. Cleaning up is what mops are for, you know."

When the yard was at last raked clear of every tiny piece of broken glass and rusty metal, the awful truth was revealed that the sandy earth and the scraggly, scrawny weeds now disclosed to view weren't a great improvement.

The Mop shook her floppy head and set them to work digging out the biggest rocks and pulling up the jimson weed, the pokeberry with its tremendous taproot, the dandelions and the horsemint and cranesbill. They left the elderberry bush with its wide, flat panicles of creamy, almond-smelling blossoms, and the butterfly weed, whose vivid orange flowers were just coming into bloom.

"They are really beautiful flowers, not weeds," said the Mop. Privately Jody thought dandelions were beautiful too, and if they were in bloom, she left them growing; but the Mop came scolding behind her and rooted them up.

Then with a garden fork borrowed from Uncle John, they dug up a garden space. And with the last of Jody's money intended for a birthday present for her father, they bought seeds and tomato plants and a bag of plant food.

This was the longest part of the operation, because it meant several trips into Wolf Town. The Mop kept remembering things they really ought to have like blue morning-glories for the porch, and reasons why they ought to make the garden plot larger, to plant beans and peas and turnips.

"I think we're going to have to do something about that Mop," said Dill grimly one hot morning as he and Jody climbed the path. "She's got to be a kind of monster. She doesn't know there is anything except work. She's worse than the Sorcerer's Apprentice's broom, because at least it did all the work. It wasn't all the time driving other people."

"Well, you've got to admit the cabin does look nice," said Jody.

"Maybe so," said Dill. "But I'm tired of working. And I've spent all my money. And Mr. Poteet will be back soon, and what are we going to tell him about what's happened to his house?"

Jody frowned. "Do you think he'll mind so

much?" she asked. "Don't you think he'll at least appreciate having a nice garden full of vegetables?"

"He hates vegetables," Dill told her fiercely. "He isn't going to like any of it. And another thing, when he comes back, what are we going to do with the Mop?"

Jody stopped still in the center of the path.

"Gosh, Dill," she whispered. "Isn't that him up ahead? Isn't that Mr. Poteet?"

Chapter Ten

The old man was walking very slowly, with his hound dog shuffling along beside him. He was loaded down. Over one arm he carried a great heap of ragged clothes. In his other hand he held a basket full of odds and ends. And on one shoulder, along with the shotgun, hung a bicycle tire. He plodded up the path, looking, as Dill said, like a walking junk heap.

For a while Jody and Dill stayed behind him, but as he drew near the cabin they hurried to catch up. It would never do for him and the Mop to come face to face alone.

"Hello, Mr. Poteet," Dill called out. The old man turned to look at them. "Well, now, howdy," he ex-

claimed. "Is that you for a fact, Dill Tracy? You
don't look much how you used to."

The children stopped in their tracks. They knew
why Dill looked different to Mr. Poteet, for on his
nose perched a pair of very strong glasses.

"I got these here store-bought glasses," he explained. "Can't say they help me see none; they
make things look plum queer. But my sister, she
bought 'em for me, said I needed 'em. And I been
a-wearin' 'em, just to please her. I can't hardly wait
to get home and take 'em off. I been away such a
spell, I do truly hanker to get back to my place."

He looked lovingly down at his basket. "But I got
a heap of things whilst I was away. This old flash-
light, see, don't need but a bulb and some batteries.
And this here bicycle tire, just got the least little
hole in it . . ."

Goodness, thought Jody. He sounds just like Dill.
And oh, dear, now that he has glasses will he be able
to tell that the Mop is a dust mop?

The Mop was inside when they got to the cabin.
It looked lovely, Jody thought, all clean and tidy,
with a neat garden to one side and morning-glory
vines beginning to twist up strings that stretched
from the ground to the porch roof. And Dill had
even propped up the porch so that it no longer
listed toward the front.

Mr. Poteet, who had been still talking about his

new possessions, now looked up and fell silent. He stared unbelievingly through his new glasses, and then he took them off and stared some more. Finally he put them back on. Jody studied his face. Surely he was pleased with what they had done. Nobody could help liking the way the cabin looked now.

"Is this my cabin?" the old man asked uncertainly. "Where—where's all my things?" He walked forward a few steps and looked dazedly around. "Where's all my good things? Where's my bottles and tires and things? And my yarbs! Who's done pulled up all my yarbs?"

His voice rose to a bellow. The Mop came slipping out of the cabin like a gray shadow. She stood on the porch, quite plainly a live dust mop.

But Mr. Poteet paid no attention to her. He dropped his bundles and rushed past her into the house. A cry of anguish sounded as he entered the door. Jody ran up and slipped her hand into the Mop's.

"I think we'd better go," she said. "I think we'd better leave."

The Mop looked confused. "What is it?" she asked weakly, and turned back toward the door.

Just then the old man roared out of the cabin like a whirlwind, and snatched up his gun. "I thought you was supposed to keep them Hadley boys out of my place," he shouted. "You worthless no-good young'uns, I'll break every bone in your bodies. I'll whup you good!"

The dog barked, the hens shrieked and cackled, the Mop squealed, and the gun went off with a blast like dynamite.

"Run," yelled Dill. "Run, Jody, run!"

Jody was ready to run. She was trembling all over. In all her life no grown person had ever screamed at her like that or threatened her so violently, and it scared her to death.

But the Mop! She couldn't leave the Mop with Mr. Poteet. Jody reached out and seized the Mop by her skinny middle, and ran for all she was worth.

She ran up the mountain. She should perhaps have run toward the path, but she didn't think of that; her legs just buzzed along in what seemed the safest direction. In her hand the Mop twisted and shook. "Put me down," she gasped. "Put me down!"

But Jody ran on heedlessly, banging the unfortunate Mop against bushes and brush. And then behind her she heard footsteps.

"Oh, oh, oh," she gasped. She twisted her head to get a glimpse of her pursuer, stumbled and nearly fell, and dropped the Mop.

The Mop tumbled into the huckleberry bushes, squeaking indignantly.

"Oh, come here, come here," entreated Jody, grabbing at her. "Hurry, hurry!"

The Mop clutched at the bushes, pulling herself out of reach. "No, no," she wailed. "I won't be carried. It's undignified. No, no!"

She struggled to her feet and scurried ahead up the shaly slope.

"Jody!" yelled Dill, behind them.

Jody didn't answer. She leaped after the Mop, and the Mop's little legs blurred as she increased her speed. Her tall body leaned dangerously forward. Suddenly her foot slipped into a crevice in the rock, she threw herself backward, there was a sudden loud snap and a faint shriek.

Jody halted and stared in horror. There lay the Mop with a great crack running slantwise almost the whole length of her handle-body.

Dill bounded up and seized one of the Mop's hands.

"Are you all right?" he cried. The Mop moaned.

"My heart," she said feebly. "My heart is broken. I shall die."

"It's not your heart," explained Dill. "You're just a little cracked."

"It is my heart," insisted the Mop. "When it comes to hearts, cracked or broken doesn't make much difference."

"But don't die," begged Jody, wringing her hands.

"I shall die if I want to," answered the Mop tartly. "I have no desire to go on living with a broken heart." And she sighed deeply and let her head flop pitifully to one side.

Jody knelt beside the Mop. "Don't die," she whimpered. "Oh, please don't die. I'd rather you be a dust mop again. Be a dust mop, oh, be a dust mop!"

On the sunlit mountainside the wind soughed and sighed in the scattered trees. Jody could hear her own breathing and Dill's. On the rocky earth between them was a dust mop, a plain ordinary dust mop with a split handle.

"Gee," whispered Dill, "you got your power back, Jody. You can work miracles again."

Jody burst into tears.

"Oh, for Pete's sake!" said Dill, standing up. "I don't see what you have to be always crying for."

Jody sobbed louder than ever. "She's dead," she sniffled. "And I liked her."

"She isn't dead, she's just a dust mop again," Dill pointed out. "She never was really alive. She was always just a sort of animated dust mop. Good grief, Jody, we've been trying all summer to get rid of her, and now we've done it and you cry."

He patted her awkwardly on the back. "I liked the old Mop too," he went on. "She was fun in a kind of awful way." He grinned. "In fact, this would have been a dull summer without her. But you had to turn her back, you know you did."

Jody wiped her face with her sleeve. "I guess so," she admitted and gulped. "But let's give her a nice funeral, Dill. I think she'd appreciate it."

Dill reflected. "I tell you what," he said slowly. "We could bury her Indian style. You know, up in a tree. I think somebody who was so crazy about nature and birds and stuff the way she was, would like that."

They found a big sugar maple tree, and Dill climbed up in it. Jody broke off some leafy sweet-smelling branches of a sassafras sapling and handed them to him. He made a sort of platform of them between two maple limbs. Jody found a long blossoming honeysuckle vine and twined it around the broken mop handle. And then she handed the dust mop up to Dill and he laid it on the bed of sassafras leaves.

"There," he said when he had climbed down. "You know that's better than going back to live in a broom closet."

Jody smiled a little. "I guess so," she said again and sat down abruptly on the ground. Suddenly she felt very tired and hungry. Dill handed her two sassafras leaves. "Turn these into something good to eat," he suggested. "Sassafras leaves are safe, I know. I eat 'em all the time."

Jody stared listlessly at the leaves. She didn't want to try it. But she would, for Dill.

She concentrated. "Be two chocolate sodas," she said slowly. And there they were in Dill's hands, two luscious-looking chocolate sodas, topped with little clouds of whipped cream and shining red cherries.

It was lovely sitting there on the side of the mountain, sipping the drinks. Jody spooned in her ice cream and began to feel more cheerful. Dill was right. The Mop had ended up in the best way possible.

"I wonder how come you can do this again," mused Dill. "Was it just getting so excited that did it for you? Or what?"

"I don't know," Jody answered. "But I haven't

tried for weeks. Maybe I could have changed the Mop back days ago, and I just didn't know it."

Dill frowned at her. "Well, that was dumb," he complained. "You should have been trying every day. All this time I might have had a motorbike and no Mop. Let's see now, when was it you ran down?"

"Right before Aunt Margaret had all that company, remember?" said Jody. "It was the day I made the motorbike and you got hurt and you said you couldn't—" She broke off suddenly. "My glasses!" she gasped. "It must be my glasses." She snatched them off and stared at them, trying to remember. "Because the ear piece got bent that morning. And then I made the Mop. And then Aunt Margaret went into Wolf Town and took my glasses with her. And all those times I *did* try to turn the Mop back, the glasses were in Wolf Town being fixed."

Dill took the ugly black-rimmed spectacles in his hand and turned them over and over. "Who would've thought it?" he murmured at last. "Here, let's prove it. We can't just leave the empty soda glasses lying around. Turn 'em back into leaves."

Jody drew her brows together as she stared at the empty soda containers Dill was holding, and thought hard about sassafras leaves. "Be leaves," she commanded, but nothing happened.

"Now put your specs back on," urged Dill.

"Don't call them specs," snapped Jody. But she slipped them on and tried once more. "Be sassafras leaves," she commanded. And Dill stood there holding two limp mitten-shaped leaves in his palms and looking rather silly.

"Wow!" he exclaimed. "To think it was as simple as that. How come we didn't figure it out sooner?"

"I don't know," said Jody. "Anyway, it doesn't matter now. Let's go home." Suddenly her hand flew to her mouth. "Mr. Poteet! What happened to him? I thought I heard him running up the mountain after us."

Dill grinned. "Not Mr. Poteet. He doesn't run anywhere. That must have been me you heard. Boy, I sort of had an idea he was going to be mad about all that cleaning up. He likes things dirty and messy; he's used to it."

Jody looked contrite. "Well, we couldn't have done anything else with the Mop in charge the way she got to be," she said thoughtfully. "And I guess I sort of agreed with her. It seemed so sad to think of him living up there all by himself, not able to see very well, and nobody to take care of him. That awful cabin and nothing to eat but moldy corn meal and sad potatoes." She brightened a little. "Maybe he'll get used to things being clean and get to like it that way."

But when they passed Mr. Poteet's cabin and

quietly retrieved the lunch basket they had left at
the edge of the clearing, she decided such a thing
would never come about. The place already had a
grimy, untidy air.

From inside the house Mr. Poteet's voice could
be heard in a steady querulous complaint. The flour-
sack curtains had been jerked from the windows.
The bicycle tires and two old jars lay in the clearing,
and the old clothes he had brought with him spilled
off the edge of the porch into the dust. The morning-glory strings had been broken, and the little
plants lay wilting in the dust.

Dill looked at Jody and grinned. "It won't take
him long to get it back into its old shape," he whispered as they turned and went on down the path.

"I'm sorry about his yarbs," said Jody. "If I'd
known they were his yarbs, maybe we could have
persuaded the Mop to leave them growing."

"Oh, those things grow all over the mountain,"
Dill reassured her. "He can find lots of them without any trouble. Besides, most of them are just
weeds and hard to get rid of. He'll probably have a
yard full of them again by the end of the summer."

He made a face. "What I hate is all that money we
put into scrub brushes and turnip seed going to
waste," he went on. "Oh, well, maybe the chickens
will enjoy the garden."

When they got back to the house, Aunt Margaret

was amazed to see them home so early. "I thought perhaps you were under some kind of spell and couldn't be seen around here while the sun was shining," she said. "You leave at daybreak and don't get back till dark practically. What's happened?"

"Nothing," said Dill. "We just got tired of playing up there. There's the mailman; I'll go get the mail."

Dill had a letter from Uncle Andrew. It had a check for ten dollars in it "for you and Jody to have fun with this summer."

"The turnip seed and some over," Dill whispered to Jody.

But Jody's letter was from Mother. Grandmother was so much better, Mother was coming to the mountains. "I want you to come to town and meet me Wednesday morning," Mother wrote. Wednesday, thought Jody. Why, that's tomorrow.

"We'll do some shopping and have lunch," the letter went on. "And I'll have a surprise for you, so be prepared."

Chapter Eleven

I wish I had had my hair cut, thought Jody as she strained to get a glimpse of her face in the tiny, dim mirror which hung over her dresser. It hadn't been cut since before she left home. And she did want to look nice for Mother.

Moreover, this blue-and-white striped dress, which had always been one of her favorites, had changed shape or something while it hung in the closet. It bunched oddly around the middle and waved up and down around her knees, too short in some places and too long in others.

But she forgot it a moment later. She was terribly excited about seeing Mother. She had been so busy the past month and so preoccupied with the Mop she really hadn't had time to remember how much she missed Mother and the others, and what a sad summer she was having.

Now as she wound down the mountain with Dill and Uncle John, she grew more and more eager. By the time the car pulled into the parking lot at the train station she was bouncing with delight.

And there was Mother! Jody flew to hug her before she was even down the steps of the Pullman car.

"Jody!" cried Mother. "How brown you are! And how you've grown. I hardly knew you."

And all Jody could do was grin.

Uncle John took Mother's baggage to the car and then he and Dill went off to the dentist, with Dill looking very mournful indeed.

"Come with me and change the dentist into a mushroom," he invited Jody in a whisper as they parted.

"I can't. You'll just have to be brave," said Jody, still grinning as she followed Mother in the opposite direction.

"As long as we're down in this neighborhood, we might as well stop in and see Dr. Green," mused Mother. "He can check your eyes now, and we won't have to bother coming to town next week."

Jody stopped dead-still, and her hand flew to her glasses. She was a little scared to let Dr. Green see them.

"Come along," urged Mother. "You'll get run

over standing in the middle of the street that way."

Dr. Green could see them in a few minutes, the nurse said. Jody waited with thumping heart. Would Dr. Green be able to tell about the miraculous lenses? He hadn't noticed anything about them when he first gave them to her. But just suppose . . .

And then the nurse said, "You can come in now, Jody."

Jody stood up and felt herself turn pale with fright. She hoped she was tan enough to hide it.

Dr. Green took off the glasses and laid them aside without even glancing at them. Jody breathed a sigh of relief.

And then there were the bright lights and the charts. Jody obediently looked through this lens and that, made a little dog jump through a hoop, and caused two red balls to become one.

"Well," said Dr. Green in an amazed tone, "that's perfect. Your glasses have worked so well I don't think you're going to need them any more."

Jody gasped and her eyes grew round. What would become of her miraculous powers? What would happen to her wonder-working glasses?

Dr. Green turned on his little revolving stool and picked up the glasses. "They did a fine job," he began admiringly—and then somehow the glasses twisted in his hand and fell to the tile floor.

"Well, well, well," murmured Dr. Green, pushing at the splintered lenses with his foot. "It certainly is fortunate you don't need them any more. Goodness me, I haven't done a trick like that in years."

Jody just stared.

A little later as they entered a department store and mounted the steps toward the floor where Girls' Sports Clothes were sold, Mother took Jody's arm and said, "Why so glum? You've looked like a thundercloud ever since we left Dr. Green's. I thought you'd be pleased about not having to wear the glasses any longer."

"Oh, yes," said Jody, trying to look cheerful. "I was glad not to have to wear them."

But I didn't want them broken, she thought dolefully. She and Dill had planned to do heaps of things with the glasses during the rest of the summer. And Daddy's birthday present—she could have gotten that with her magic powers.

Most important, she had had a secret plan to make herself, well, not beautiful, but an improvement over fat, plain Joan Ransom. She had those horrid black frames off her nose, of course, she thought as she followed Mother over the thickly carpeted floor, but she had meant to do much more than that. It was dreadful to be still the old dumpy way she was, when she could have been, by using the glasses, tall and thin and brown and interesting-looking, like that girl over there. The one with the too-long hair and the too-short dress, the girl with the woman who looked like Mo—

Jody gaped and the girl in the mirror gaped back. Slowly Jody moved toward her reflection. Six weeks and lots of hard work in the sun had worked a sort of miracle of their own. For the girl in the mirror was tall and tanned and quite definitely slender.

If there had been a good looking-glass in her room at Aunt Margaret's, she might have seen this happening. But there'd only been that little spotted one high up over her head, and she'd only looked in it enough to see if her hair part was straight.

"Will navy blue shorts do, or would you like plaid?" asked Mother from behind her.

"Navy's fine," said Jody dreamily. "Or plaid, either one."

"You're a help," said Mother.

In the restaurant Jody ordered a tomato stuffed with shrimp salad, her very favorite. And for dessert she was contemplating the blissful advantages of pecan pie over lemon cream tart, or vice versa, when Mother said, "And now for the surprise."

Jody had forgotten the surprise. In fact, she had

had so many surprises in the past few days, she didn't know whether she could stand another one. She looked at her mother cautiously.

"We're going to spend another week or so in the mountains," said Mother. "And by that time Steve's camp will be over. So you and Steve and I are going to the beach. Roger will come there after a few days. And we're not sure, but we think Daddy will get home in time to spend the last two weeks with us too."

"Oh, Mother!" cried Jody. "Oh, wonderful. Oh, beautiful!"

Mother smiled. "There's just one other thing," she said. "And maybe you won't like it so much. But I thought we'd take Dill with us, if he'll come."

Jody was amazed. "Not like it," she exclaimed. "Why, that makes it perfect. I'd hate to leave Dill."

"I thought you and Dill didn't get along so well," explained Mother.

"Why—why—" said Jody in bewilderment. But, of course, Mother was right. She didn't get along with Dill. And then she grinned. "I found out a lot about Dill this summer," she confessed. "He isn't being mean. He's just being friendly."

And in the car late that afternoon, twisting back up into the cooler scented air of the mountains, Jody thought about all she'd discovered during the summer. About Dill, who was really the friendliest sort of person. About Mr. Poteet, who found living in loneliness and disarray exactly the sort of life that suited him. About the Mop, who was only a dust mop and yet who had managed to change a summer for a good many people, whose little eyes and invisible ears could hear and see so much and point it out for human eyes and ears.

Jody frowned. The Mop and all that concerned her seemed so far away and long ago compared to here and now and all the solid joys that lay before her, the sunny beach and the ocean and the fun of being with all her family. Maybe she'd just imagined that about the Mop and the glasses and working miracles. Had all those things really happened?

Maybe they hadn't. When she'd finally got a chance to tell Dill the sad news about the glasses, he hadn't seemed a bit upset. In fact, he hadn't seemed to know quite what she was talking about.

"Gosh, it doesn't matter, does it?" he had asked. "Aren't your eyes all right? Gosh, Jody, we're going to the beach!"

So perhaps she had invented it all in her head, made up the Mop and her funny arms and legs and her imperious ways. But no, she couldn't have made up the Mop any more than she could have made up Mr. Poteet and his awful cabin.

But of course she *had* made up the Mop when she brought her to life. Jody's head began to whirl.

She pushed her face up close to the window to smell the fresh mountain air. A light rain had begun to fall, hardly more than a heavy mist, and farther up the road fog swelled and billowed in the curves. The trees along the highway looked washed and green; on their dark trunks the pale lichens glistened.

And suddenly above the sound of the car's engine she heard the lovely and mysterious bird song she had heard that day beside the creek. Why, there must be thousands of those birds. One was singing

in every bend of the road, the silvery fluting song
that swirled down and down and then began again.

"Listen," said Uncle John. "The veeries are really
enjoying the rain. They hardly ever sing this late
in the summer unless there's an afternoon shower
like this. I love to hear them."

A veery! Jody told herself. Of course, she should
have known. Veery was what it said, vee-eee-e-ree—
vee-eee-rree—veee-eee-rrree . . .

But to think, Uncle John had known all along.
If only she'd thought to ask him, she wouldn't have
had to take the Mop's word that it was a fruit-
frosted cupcake.

On the front seat Dill suddenly sat up straight.

"Happy at the ocean,
Happy at the beach,
Happy at the ocean,
Happy as a peach,"

he sang loudly. "Isn't that beautiful? I made it up
myself."

"Its elegance and charm render me absolutely
speechless," answered Uncle John. "But just how
happy is a peach?"

"Awful happy," answered Dill.

Jody giggled. Who needed magic glasses? She and
Dill had plenty of fun without them. And the world
was a wonderful place, full of beautiful and exciting

things, a place where you could get your heart's desire without even knowing you were doing it.

"Happy at the ocean," caroled Dill, and Jody
joined in:

"Happy as a peach!"

ABOUT THE AUTHOR

Wilson Gage is the pen name of Mary Q. Steele, one of a family of gifted and successful writers; her husband, William, her sister, and her mother, Christine Govan, are the authors of many popular books for children and young people.

Wilson Gage was born in Chattanooga, Tennessee, and is a graduate of the University of Chattanooga where she received a bachelor's degree in physics and mathematics. Her long interest in nature—for which she confesses an "unathletic" love—and in regional history has characterized all of her books, most recently *Dan and the Miranda* and *A Wild Goose Tale*. She has three children and lives in Signal Mountain, Tennessee.